W9-BZB-430

# and the Alpha Centauri 5000

Poog

Gax

Akiko

Mr. Beeba

Spuckler

# and the Alpha Centauri 5000

Written and illustrated by

## MARK CRILLEY

DELACORTE PRESS

Published by
Delacorte Press
an imprint of
Random House Children's Books
a division of Random House, Inc.
New York

Visit us on the Web! www.randomhouse.com/kids
Educators and librarians, for a variety of teaching tools, visit us at
www.randomhouse.com/teachers

Library of Congress Cataloging-in-Publication Data
Crilley, Mark.
    Akiko and the Alpha Centauri 5000 / Mark Crilley.
        p.   cm.
    Sequel to: Akiko in the Castle of Alia Rellapor.
    Summary: Akiko's spaceship race from one side of the galaxy to
the other is complicated when Spuckler discovers that an old rival
of his is also competing.
    ISBN 0-385-72969-3 (trade)
    [1. Science fiction.   2. Adventure and adventurers—Fiction.
3. Japanese Americans—Fiction.]   I. Title.
    PZ7.C869275 Ac 2003
    [Fic]—dc21                                    2002006767

The text of this book is set in 15-point Centaur.

Printed in the United States of America

March 2003

10 9 8 7 6 5 4 3 2 1
BVG

*To three good friends:*
*Dennis Moylan, Thom Powers, and John Walter*

This book might never have made it across the finish line if not for the expert navigating skills of my editor, Jennifer Wingertzahn, who was always near the dashboard when I needed her, pointing out the asteroids and telling me when I had the map upside down. Special thanks to others who have worked behind the scenes to get Akiko to where she is today: Joe Monti, Ridge Rooms, Robb Horan, Larry Salamone, Mark Bellis, Melissa Knight, and Colleen Fellingham. As always I send hugs and kisses to my wife, Miki, and son, Matthew.

# Chapter 1

**My name is Akiko.** This is the story of how I went from building a snowman to flying through a black hole to nearly getting crushed by the Jaws of—

Well, I don't want to give it all away.

Let's just say for now that some really weird stuff happened to me the other day. Stuff involving my friends from the planet Smoo, a big rusty spaceship named *Boach's Bullet*, and several tons of something green and smelly called grull.

See what I mean? *Weird stuff.*

I'll start with the snowman.

It was a freezing cold January morning, a Saturday. My best friend, Melissa, and I were playing in Middleton Park, just a few blocks from the apartment building where we both live. We were chucking snowballs at each other, making sorry-looking igloos, and just generally goofing around with the six or seven inches of snow that had fallen the night before.

"Middleton is nowhere," said Melissa. "When I grow up I'm moving to a big city. Where exciting stuff happens. Every day, all the time. And I'll tell everyone I meet: Stay away from Middleton. Unless you really like being bored."

"Oh, come on," I said. "It's not *that* bad."

Melissa chucked a snowball and we both watched it slide across the frozen duck pond. I threw one too, but it didn't go as far.

"Trust me, Akiko. I've been to Chicago and Milwaukee and Cincinnati. Those are *real* cities. Your problem is you've never been away from your own hometown."

(Melissa's problem is she starts too many sentences with "Your problem is.")

"I have too," I said.

"Where have you been?"

"I've been to places you've never even *heard* of."

"Such as?"

2

If only I could tell her: *Smoo! Quilk! The castle of Alia Rellapor!*

"Leamington."

"*Leamington?*" She laughed and shook her head. "I've been to Leamington. It's even worse than Middleton." She threw another snowball. "When I get older I'm going to stay away from any place that ends with -*ton.*"

"I *like* Leamington," I said. "My gramma lives there."

"You like everything," Melissa said. "That's your whole problem."

Then Melissa's mom called her from the top of a hill on the other side of the duck pond.

"Come on, 'Liss! Time to go!"

"But Mom," she said, "we're in the middle of something really important here."

Ha!

"Count of ten: one . . . two . . ."

"Mom!" Melissa pleaded. She stretched it out until it sounded like *Maaaah-um.*

". . . three . . . four . . ."

"Gotta go." Melissa sighed, dropped the snowball

she'd been making, and trotted off around the edge of the duck pond. I stood there and watched the puffs of breath trail off behind her.

"See ya, Melissa!"

"See ya!"

A minute later there was no one in the park but me.

I was about to head back home, but then I decided to make a snowman. We don't get that much snow in Middleton, so there are only so many chances for snowman making before it's suddenly March and the so-called snow is so gray and slushy you don't want your mittens going anywhere *near* it.

I had finished with the second big ball of snow— the snowman's belly—and was working on the third when I began to feel warm. *Seriously* warm. It was like I was being heated from inside or something. I unzipped my coat and loosened my scarf a little, but it didn't really help. I took off my mittens and stuffed them in my coat pockets.

That's when it started happening.

First my hand-knit winter hat disappeared. It sort of loosened itself from my head like it was, I don't know, *letting go* of me. And then it just vanished. By that point I was feeling downright feverish. I reached into my coat to loosen my scarf a little more and found that it had disappeared too.

"Uh-oh."

Then my eyes went haywire. All of Middleton Park started to lose its color. The black tree trunks faded to gray and then to white, all the buildings turned white, and the sky turned white: I could hardly see anything but white, no matter what direction I turned.

There was a surge of heat from inside me, like a burst of flame right between my heart and my stomach.

*DOP!*

   *DADA-DOP!*

      *DADA-DOP-DOP-DOP!*

A popping noise shot through my skull from one ear to the other, and when I looked down . . . I couldn't see my *body* anymore! Everything around me got whiter and whiter until I was surrounded by a million little white-hot suns and I had to shut my eyes and throw my hands over them and . . .

*FFLAAAAAAAAAM!*

There was a terrific slamming sound, louder than anything I'd ever heard in my life.

*FLA-FFLLLAAAAAAAAAAAAMMM!*

A second sound, even louder. Then:

Total silence.

*zzzzzzzzzzzzzz*

Except for a low, buzzing hum in my head.

I uncovered my eyes.

I was kneeling in the middle of a large gray square, smooth and glossy, but with scuff marks all over it like a well-used floor. Middleton Park was gone, replaced by a sea of blackness in all directions. Well, *most* of Middleton Park was gone, anyway. My now half-melted snowman was still right there in front of me, for some reason.

The humming slowly

gave way to a loud rattling noise, like an old muffler in need of repair. There was a flicker of light, then all at once everything snapped into focus: I was in a small room cluttered with all sorts of strange machines and flashing orange lights. On one side of the room was a large glass windshield, beyond which lay a field of stars.

I was inside a spaceship.

"Wait! Look!" said a familiar voice just behind me. "That's her! She's coming through!"

"You're a lucky man, Beebs," said a second voice, just as familiar. "Let's hope her innards didn't get flipped upside down."

I spun around and found myself face to face with my Smoovian friends, Spuckler and Mr. Beeba. They were crouching just beyond the edge of the square, staring at me with wide eyes. Behind them to the left was Spuckler's rusty robot, Gax, and hovering above Gax was Poog in all his strange purple-round glory.

Mr. Beeba flinched and pointed behind me.

"Good heavens!" he cried. "She's not alone! We've picked up some sort of *alien ice creature!*"

"Don't worry, Beebs," said Spuckler, eyeing the

unfinished snowman. "It ain't breathin'. I think the Trans-Moovulator musta killed it."

"What . . . ," I started.

"How…"

I paused.

Took a deep breath.

*"Where am I?"*

# Chapter 2

"**Relax, Akiko,**" said Mr. Beeba. "There will be plenty of time for explanations later. . . ."

"No no no no no!" I said. "I want the explanations now. *Right* now."

Mr. Beeba and Spuckler glanced at each other. Gax rattled a bit, and Poog smiled apologetically.

"We *needed* ya, 'Kiko," said Spuckler. "And there jus' wasn't *time* to send ya a letter. . . ."

"We'll put you *right* back where you were, dear girl," Mr. Beeba said, fiddling with his puffy gloved fingers. "Just as soon as we're finished."

A few feet behind Mr. Beeba's head was a wall with a round glass portal in it, like something salvaged from an abandoned submarine. Judging by the stars racing by beyond it, we were moving at an incredible speed.

"As soon as we're finished with *what?*"

"I *TOLD* THEM IT WASN'T A GOOD IDEA!" Gax said, his mechanical voice high-pitched and tinny. "I TOLD THEM IT WOULD ONLY MAKE YOU ANGRY. . . ."

Poog, who had been silent until now, blurted out a few syllables in his warbly, gurgly language. I assumed he was agreeing with Gax.

"Okay. Answer time! What's going on here?"

"Look, 'Kiko." Spuckler dragged a hand through his spiky blue hair. "It's real simple. There's this big rocket-ship race, ya see, goin' from one side of the universe to the other—"

"An unconscionable misrepresentation of the facts," Mr. Beeba told me. "It runs only 7/29 of the way at most. The promoters, however, would *love* to have you believe otherwise."

I blinked and said nothing. I figured the longer I let them talk, the better the chances of them saying something that made sense.

"Th' first rocket ship to make it 'cross the finish line

wins the Centauri Cup," Spuckler continued. "And I reckon we got that cup just about in the bag s'long as we get this here spaceship's Hurlix 'Puter programmed right."

The odds of them making sense were starting to look slim.

"Tragically," said Mr. Beeba, "the programming manual Spuckler bought—"

"Secondhand, for five gilpots," Spuckler whispered with a wink.

"—is written in an alien tongue that I am quite unable to read," Mr. Beeba said. "A spectacularly rare occurrence, mind you. I got my doctorate in interplanetary linguistics, you know."

Spuckler continued: "So it turns out your home planet ain't more'n a hop, skip, and a jump from the startin' line." He signaled with a finger that this was where *I* came in. "And with the race beginnin' in just another half an hour, we didn't have *time* to pick y'up the usual way."

I kept blinking. They kept talking.

"As luck would have it, this ship is equipped with a Trans-Moovulator." Mr. Beeba pointed at a two-foot-square box nearby. It was covered with dials and wheezed loudly every few seconds like a coffeemaker. "I trust the trip from Earth to this ship wasn't too unpleasant for you."

I stood there staring at Spuckler and Mr. Beeba for a

good half-minute. Their explanation—if that's what you want to call it—was apparently finished.

"Let me get this straight," I said. "You guys are competing in some big rocket-ship race . . ."

Mr. Beeba and Spuckler nodded in unison.

". . . and you've got some sort of manual you can't read . . ."

They nodded again.

". . . and for some reason you thought *I* might be able to help you . . ."

Another nod.

". . . and so you just *beamed* me up here without even warning me!"

"*Beamed* is such a crude word, Akiko," Mr. Beeba said. "We Trans-Moovulated you."

"I don't care *what* word you use!" I cried. "You guys can't just snatch me up off the face of the Earth any time you feel like it!"

There was a brief pause.

"Oh, but we can," Mr. Beeba said. "You see, that's the marvelous thing about Trans-Moovulation technology—"

"Okay, you can. Obviously you can. You just *did*."

I was getting warm again, only this time it was from good old-fashioned anger.

"But . . . ," I continued, pointing a very pointy finger first at Mr. Beeba, then at Spuckler, ". . . don't expect me to be *happy* about it."

# Chapter 3

**The spaceship rattled** past the stars as Gax mopped up the melted remains of my snowman. Spuckler was seated at the front of the ship, steering us through a field of whirling pink asteroids. Mr. Beeba invited me to sit down on a passenger seat that folded out from one of the walls. He then brought me a glass filled with a brownish gray sludge that was supposed to ease the effects of being Trans-Moovulated. By the time I'd finished swigging it down—it wasn't half bad, actually—I was starting to get used to the idea that I'd be spending the next few hours helping Spuckler and Mr. Beeba in their quest to win the Centauri Cup. It was a Saturday in January. What *else* was I going to do?

"I still don't get it. What does this unreadable manual have to do with *me?*"

"Well, Akiko," Mr. Beeba answered, "it just so happens that the text in question was published on the planet Jabble." He said this last word as if he fully expected me to recognize it, as if there was no need to say anything else.

He reached into a nearby drawer, pulled out a thick, dog-eared manual, and carefully opened it. He placed it in front of me. The words on the page were squared off and criss-crossed with intricate lines. Actually, they didn't even look like words. They were more like computer chips.

"Well?" said Mr. Beeba.

I scratched the back of my neck. "Am I supposed to be able to read this, Mr. B.?"

"Not *all* of it! My word, no, certainly not. But I do distinctly recall your telling me—and I never forget something like this—that both of your parents are of Jabblenese descent and that as a result you know a fair amount of the language yourself."

My jaw dropped.

"Jabblenese? *Jabblenese?*" I said. It was all I could do to stop from smacking my forehead like a guy in an old movie. "My parents aren't Jabblenese! They're *Jap*anese!"

Mr. Beeba said nothing. He was still smiling, for some reason.

"You mean they're from the planet *Japa?*"

"My parents are from the planet *Earth!* They can't read Jabblenese, and neither can I!"

There was a very long pause, during which Mr. Beeba did nothing but stare at me. His smile had vanished, and now his lips were puckered into a little O-shaped hole.

"Oh dear."

He closed the manual, put it in the drawer, then turned back to me and stared a little more.

"Well, it's nothing to be *ashamed* of, Akiko," he said

at last. "I'm sure you'd pick up the language quickly enough if you had a good Jabblenese tutor."

"Don't worry, 'Kiko," said Spuckler. "I've flown this ship loadsa times without even usin' the Hurlix 'Puter. It'll be tricky, but we'll scrape by without it."

With all the pink asteroids zipping past, some of them missing us by just a few yards, I didn't like the idea of being inside a ship that was scraping by.

"So, uh, what exactly does the Hurlix Computer do?"

"Makes the ship easier t' steer," Spuckler explained. "When you ain't got her programmed right, you hafta do everything manually."

I looked at the countless knobs, buttons, lights, and levers that covered the dashboard. It wasn't something I'd want to deal with manually. It wasn't something I'd want to deal with at *all*.

"How did you ever learn to fly this thing?" I asked.

"Trial an' error, 'Kiko. Trial an'—"

*KRRRAAAAAASH!*

Suddenly the ship jerked to one side, sending Mr. Beeba and me rolling wildly across the floor. Poog darted along after me, and Gax, with great difficulty, wheeled himself over to Spuckler's side.

"Sorry, gang, hit an asteroid there," Spuckler called out as he tried to get the spaceship level. "That won't happen agai—"

*FWWAAAAAMM!*

"Dagnabbit!"

This time the ship flipped completely upside down, and Mr. Beeba, Gax, and I flew through the air and tumbled across the ceiling, which for all practical purposes was now the floor. Something hit me hard in the head—possibly one of Gax's spare parts—and made a loud twanging noise as it bounced off and spun away into the darkness.

Spuckler, who had strapped himself into the driver's seat, was just as upside down as the rest of the ship. He didn't even seem to notice, actually. He was too busy punching buttons and pulling levers, weaving us through the cloud of asteroids that now surrounded us.

"Man, this is gonna slow us down," Spuckler said, sounding like a trucker stuck in traffic. "All the best places on the starting line'll be nabbed by the time we get there."

"Never mind the starting line, you idiot!" Mr. Beeba shouted. "Get this ship right side up again!"

"Right side down, inside up," said Spuckler as we zoomed beneath one particularly massive asteroid, "I don't see what the heck difference it makes."

"Please, Spuckler!" I cried, holding on to a ceiling lamp for dear life, "I'm getting seasick."

"You mean *space*sick, 'Kiko," said Spuckler.

"Quite right," said Mr. Beeba. "Unless you meant to use the phrase *metaphorically,* of course."

*"Whatever!"* I yelled.

"All right, all right." Spuckler gave the steering wheel an abrupt jerk and sent all of us flying back to the floor. This time I landed squarely on my butt, and Mr. Beeba flopped right down on top of me. He mumbled an apology as he pulled himself off.

*PWWWAAAAAMM!*

"Okay, gang," said Spuckler as the ship shook from yet another collision. "I think that's the last of 'em."

*TWWAAM!*

"'Cept for that one."

Sure enough, the pink asteroids had disappeared

from view and the ship was now sailing smoothly through the stars. Poog smiled and made a series of garbled gurgles, which Mr. Beeba translated as follows:

"It won't be long now. The starting line is only ten minutes away at most."

The brush with the asteroids inspired me to take one last stab at talking my way out of this.

"Look, guys," I said, "I can't read Jabblenese, so you don't really *need* me to be here."

"Yeah, ya got a point there, 'Kiko," Spuckler replied after a moment.

"Indeed," Mr. Beeba said, "you're entirely super-fluous at this stage in the game, there's no getting around that."

"Okay, okay, don't rub it in," I said. "The point is, why don't you just beam me back to Earth—"

"TRANS-MOOVULATE YOU BACK TO EARTH," said Gax.

"Yeah, right, moovulate me back to Earth, zap me back to Earth, whatever it takes. Then you can do the race without me. A ship with fewer people in it goes faster, right?"

"Sorry, 'Kiko," Spuckler said. "We're outta range

now. Best we could do is Trans-Moovulate'cha back to somewhere near the edge of the Milky Way. Then you'd hafta try'n' *hitch* your way back home."

"Highly inadvisable, Akiko," Mr. Beeba said. "That area of the Milky Way has really gone to seed lately. There's no telling what sort of riffraff you'd find hanging about."

I pictured myself standing in the middle of some alien desert with my thumb stuck out. Suddenly, joining them in the race didn't seem like such a bad idea.

I pulled my watch out of my pocket. It was 11 A.M.

"Just one thing," I said. "You've got to get me back to Earth before dinnertime. My parents will start to worry."

# Chapter 4

A few minutes later we arrived at the starting gate of the Alpha Centauri 5000. It was a huge open-air space station about a mile long but not very wide, like an aircraft carrier floating among the stars. There were small spectator-filled grandstands on either end, with the rest

of the surface given over to ten sleek rocket ships, most of them covered in shiny chrome. They were all facing the same direction, parked neatly behind a thick white line that ran the entire length of the platform.

"Platinum's *in* this year," said Spuckler. "Looks like we're gonna be the only ones with personality round here."

Gax clicked and buzzed his agreement.

Spuckler steered the ship in for a landing on one of the few remaining spots and killed the engine. Pulling a knob on the dashboard, he popped open a door in a nearby wall. The clean and quiet air of our ship was immediately overtaken by revving engines and exhaust fumes. I spent the next few minutes trying to plug my ears and my nose at the same time. Spuckler encouraged us to get out and stretch our legs. (He must not have been talking to Poog and Gax, since they have no legs to stretch.)

"Once the race gets started there won't be time for dawdlin'," he said as he leaped out the door, "so y'all might as well dawdle while the dawdlin's good!"

Mr. Beeba and I stepped carefully out into the

strange noisy world surrounding us. Multi-antennaed aliens dashed back and forth carrying oddly shaped wrenches and crates full of freshly oiled spare parts. Silvery androids beeped and bleated as they made last-minute repairs on the wings of ships high above us. Rocket engines backfired repeatedly, each followed by a series of unintelligible cries from their respective owners—alien cussing, I'll bet. It was definitely not my kind of hangout.

"I really should have brought more reading material along," Mr. Beeba said as he strolled away, followed closely by Poog. "I wonder if anyone's left any scientific journals lying about."

I was so busy taking in all the sights and sounds I almost forgot to turn around and look at our own ship, which until now I'd only viewed from the inside. Once I did see it, I kind of wished I could *unsee* it. Ours was just about the rustiest, clunkiest, all-around junkiest ship of them all. It was brown and orange with charcoal-colored stains all over the place, and here and there big sheets of scrap steel had been hammered haphazardly into place: jagged-edged patches that looked like they had been torn out of abandoned space cars, tin roofs, vending machines—whatever Spuckler had managed to lay his hands on. The whole thing was supported by three wheels, each a different size and color, and one almost entirely deflated. It looked as if a single nudge would cause the entire ship to collapse back into the pile of rubbish it had been constructed from.

"Purty, ain't she?" Spuckler stroked his jaw like a proud skipper. "Built her m'self, believe it or not."

"No way!" I said, trying my best to sound as if I hadn't already come to that conclusion several minutes earlier.

"Oh yeah, 'Kiko. Pounded 'er together with my own two hands." He pulled out a filthy rag and rubbed away a stain on the ship's hull that must have struck him as less appealing than the other stains around it. "Take it from me, little lady. If you want somethin' done right, ya gotta do it 'cherself."

FLOOOOOOOOOOOOOOOOOOOOT!

A loud, high-pitched horn blast echoed across the space station, followed by a staticky announcement in several alien languages.

"Only a minute to go," Spuckler said as he dashed back behind the engine.

"SIR, ONE OF THE ASTEROIDS MADE A HOLE IN THE ROOF," Gax said from somewhere above us. "I'M AFRAID IT WILL REQUIRE SEVERAL MORE MINUTES TO BE PROPERLY REPAIRED."

"We ain't *got* sev'ral minutes, Gax!" Spuckler said. "How big is it?"

"APPROXIMATELY 5.8 INCHES IN DIAMETER, SIR."

"Here, stick *this* in it." Spuckler tossed something soft and gray up to Gax. "That'll hold her at least till we get to Gorda Glassdok." Was that the same oily rag

I'd seen him using just a minute ago? I decided I didn't really want to know.

*FLOOOOOOOOOOOOOOOOOOOT!*

Assuming the second horn blast meant there were only thirty seconds left, I reboarded the ship and buckled myself into one of the seats. A moment later Mr. Beeba came bustling in, a stack of oil-stained books tucked under each arm. Poog floated after him, his mouth curved into an amused smile.

"Engine-maintenance manuals," Mr. Beeba said as he adjusted his safety-belt straps. "Not my ideal form of literature, of course. But it'll do in a pinch, I suppose."

Gax lowered himself back into the ship through a

passageway in the ceiling, which appeared to have been cut especially for him. He then scooted over to a spot on the floor, where he locked himself down like a boot snapping into a ski.

*FLOO-FLOOOOT!*

"Fifteen seconds!" Mr. Beeba said as the revving of engines outside rose to a roar.

"Well, of all the dagnabbed ding-dang . . ." Spuckler's voice echoed with tin-can hollowness from a vent in the wall. It sounded like he was repairing the engine—or, more likely, failing to repair it—from the inside.

"Spuckler, you idiot!" Mr. Beeba cried. "Get your flabby little tush inside here!" (Spuckler's tush was not the least bit flabby, actually. But, hey. People say funny things when they're under pressure.)

*KLAANK!*

There was a loud metallic noise that I figured was something getting whacked with a wrench out of pure frustration. A moment later Spuckler hurled himself through the door, somersaulting in midair and landing squarely in the driver's seat. It was a pretty cool move, I have to admit.

"Five seconds!" Mr. Beeba said.

Spuckler punched madly at buttons all over the dashboard, like an organist gone insane.

"Four!"

Our ship's engine finally rumbled to life, causing the walls to vibrate with tooth-chattering intensity.

"Three!"

Spuckler lurched violently to one side and yanked a big brass knob. A spritz of blue wiper fluid splattered across the windshield and began oozing down slowly.

"Two!"

*"Dagnabbit!"* Spuckler said, apparently unable to get the wipers to work.

I reached down and gripped the edge of my seat as tightly as I could.

"One!"

*BLA-BLAAAAAAAM!*

The engine exploded into high gear, sucking the ship backward for a moment, then shooting us all forward at breakneck speed.

*VOOOOOOOOOOOOT!*

Somewhere beneath all the competing noises I heard

a final trumpet blast, and with that we rocketed over the edge of the platform, veering unsteadily off to the left before joining the pack of shimmering spaceships surrounding us.

The Alpha Centauri 5000 had begun.

# Chapter 5

**Within seconds we fell** to the back of the group, and with each passing minute the other ships moved farther ahead of us.

"We need more grull!" Spuckler said as he pulled a lever on the dashboard.

"More grull?" asked Mr. Beeba. "Already? But we've only just started!"

"That's right," said Spuckler, "and we ain't never gonna get anywhere near the front of this pack if you don't start shovelin' grull, and I mean like right-now-*pronto!*"

Mr. Beeba grabbed a shovel from underneath his seat and Gax slid open a door in one of the walls near the back of the ship, revealing a large compartment filled with angular dark green pellets.

"I thought the plan was to conserve our grull until we reached Gorda Glassdok," said Mr. Beeba as he thrust the shovel into the compartment and loaded it with pellets.

"Change of plans, Beebs." Spuckler yanked a knob that caused a dome-shaped portion of the floor to pop open just inches from Mr. Beeba's feet.

*SP'SSSSSSSSSSSSSSSSHHHHH!*

Flames shot up from the hole, nearly touching the ceiling. The entire room quickly grew as hot as a sauna. Mr. Beeba tossed in several shovelfuls of the green pellets.

*B'SSSSSSSSSHHHH!*

The flames leaped higher and my nostrils filled with a horrible burned-plastic kind of odor: the soon-to-be-familiar stink of burning grull.

"More!" said Spuckler.

"But—"

"*More,* I said!"

Mr. Beeba sighed and fed another shovelful of grull into the flames.

"That's the stuff!"

Then another . . .

"Stop scrimpin'!"

. . . and another . . .

"Don't get stingy on me, Beebs!"

. . . and several more, until finally Mr. Beeba dropped the shovel in exhaustion and kicked the lid back over the flames. Gax raced over to monitor a glass-covered dial on the wall.

*GUDDA-GUDDA-GUDDA-GOOOOOOM!*

The whole ship rocked from side to side and the floor shook beneath our feet. A drawer full of tools near Spuckler's side rattled open, coughing its contents onto the floor, where they clattered from one end of the ship to the other. My safety belts dug into my stomach as I slid several inches toward the back of the ship. Whatever this grull was made of, it certainly packed a punch.

"Whuh-*hooooooh!*" shouted Spuckler. "Comin' through, folks!"

We passed spaceships left and right, eventually settling into a position near the front of the pack: nine ships behind us and just one ahead.

"That's more like it," said Spuckler. "Front and center's the only place for *Boach's Bullet!*"

"'*Boach's Bullet*'?" I asked Mr. Beeba, who had just strapped himself into the seat beside me with great difficulty.

"A perfectly dreadful name for a spaceship, don't you think?" he replied. "I lobbied very hard for the *Gossamer Galleon*, but to no avail."

Poog floated forward to Spuckler, opened his little mouth, and let out a series of high-pitched gurgling noises. He looked a little worried.

"Poog says we are now approaching the Labyrinth of Lulla-ma-Waygo," translated Mr. Beeba.

"Great!" said Spuckler. "One down, two t' go!"

"You mean *none* down," Mr. Beeba said. "We haven't made it *through* the Labyrinth yet."

"The glaaaahss is aaahlways haahlf empty, Spuck-laaah," Spuckler said, doing his best impression of Mr. Beeba, "nevaaah haahlf full!" It was actually a pretty lousy impression, but I got the general idea.

"What's this about a labyrinth?" I asked.

"Racin' straight from one side of the universe to the other'd be as dull as dishwater, 'Kiko," Spuckler explained, "so they tossed in a few hurdles along the way, jus' to make it a challenge."

Mr. Beeba cleared his throat and laid a hand on my arm. "The Labyrinth of Lulla-ma-Waygo is a uniquely structured planetary entity. Solar currents and various electromagnetic phenomena have, over a period of many millennia, sculpted its surface into an enormous maze of limestone and graphite."

"Every ship's gotta get through the maze before car-ryin' on to the next parta the race," Spuckler said. "The trick is to go as fast as you can without crashin' into too much stuff. Don't worry, though," he added, "*Boach's Bullet's* crashed hunnerds of times and it ain't never fallen apart once."

"That's very reassuring," I said.

"Ain't it, though?" replied Spuckler, stroking the dashboard proudly.

# Chapter 6

**A minute later** the Labyrinth of Lulla-ma-Waygo came into view. It was a lovely pale shade of moss green, spinning on a gently tilted axis. The closer we got to it, though, the more frightening it became. Every square foot of the landscape was cut into narrow valleys and mountain ranges, with countless gorges and gullies

twisting off in all directions. I swallowed hard and hoped that *Boach's Bullet* would be able to withstand one or two more crashes.

"OUR CURRENT TRAJECTORY WILL CAUSE US TO OVERSHOOT THE ENTRANCE," announced Gax.

"Don't fret, buddy," Spuckler replied, steering the ship into a nosedive. "This way is funner."

*"More fun,"* said Mr. Beeba.

"Comin' right up!" Spuckler pulled a lever near the floor, instantly doubling our speed.

We were now rocketing straight down toward a huge opening in the surface of the planet. There was a mass of flashing lights in the shape of an arrow directing all the ships into the hole. I dug my fingers into the upholstery of my seat, preparing for what I figured would be the most horrifying roller-coaster ride of my ten-year-old life.

I was wrong.

It was a lot worse than that.

*Boach's Bullet* shot into the hole and immediately veered off to the left, then the right, then the left again, then up, down, back, forth, sideways, inways, outways, and everywhichways as Spuckler steered us through a series of hair-raisingly narrow passages. The sides of cliffs blurred into a pale green haze as we raced by, often so close that it felt like we were skidding across them like a stone skipping over water.

Within minutes I was feeling extremely queasy, and it was all I could do to keep the pancakes I'd had for breakfast that morning (back on Earth! It seemed so long ago now!) from coming right back up the way they'd gone down. Mr. Beeba looked unwell too, and Poog had a very troubled expression on his face. Even Gax looked like he was beginning to question his unquestioning faith in his master's flying abilities. Only

Spuckler remained thoroughly chipper, singing a sea chantey—I guess it was a *space* chantey, actually—as he sent the ship careening through one unbearably tight squeeze after another.

*"Oh, there ain't no life like a life in space,*
*Where there ain't no strife and I knows my place,*
*And I'll take first place in this gol-durned raaaaaaace,*
*Oady-hoady oady-hoady ode-alooooo . . ."*

It was the sort of tune you found pretty annoying the first time, really annoying the second time, and by the fifteenth time you were about ready to strangle the man, I swear.

He was doing an excellent job of steering, though. No matter how rough the ride got, no matter how certain it seemed that we'd *never* make it through that next gap, we always came through all right. After a few minutes I relaxed my grip on the edge of my seat and started to breathe like something approaching normal.

I should have known it was too good to last.

*SKRRREEEEEEEEEEEEEETTCHHH!*

Spuckler was pulling on four different knobs at once, heaving his body backward. The whole ship rattled and shook, and the tools that had spilled out of the drawer earlier came dancing back across the floor. Bit by bit the vibrations grew less jarring and the high-pitched scream of the engines died down to a low, steady rumble.

There in front of the windshield stood a solid wall of pale green stone, not more than a foot beyond the nose of our ship. If Spuckler had put on the brakes even a second later, we'd all have been done for. I had this sudden vivid picture in my head of spitballs permanently plastered to the wall of my Middleton Elementary homeroom.

"Dead end," said Spuckler. He threw the engine into reverse.

A ship roared by somewhere in the distance.

Spuckler turned *Boach's Bullet* around and retraced our path, eventually taking us into an entirely different gorge. He seemed to be flying the ship even more recklessly than before, probably trying to make up the time we'd lost turning around. Judging by the roar of our engines, we were nearly back to our original speed. Then . . .

*SKRRREEEEEEEEEE-*

**PAAAAAAAAAASSSH!**

# Chapter 7

Objects of all shapes and sizes tumbled through the air. The safety belts dug into my sides so deeply I thought I was going to bleed. I covered my head with my arms but wound up banging it on the wall anyway. One of my shoes nearly came off.

"Dagnab the *dingle-hoffer!*" cried Spuckler.

We now found ourselves face to face with another wall of stone, this time having crashed right into it. All the lights in the ship went out for about five seconds, then unsteadily flashed back on again, revealing spare parts and loose grull spilled all over the floor, along with nearly every door to every compartment now open and swinging back and forth like loose window shutters. There was also a good-sized crack in the

windshield. (A *new* one, I should say, since there had been several from the start.)

"WE'VE CRASHED, SIR," said Gax.

"I know we've crashed!" Spuckler hollered. "I'm the guy who did the *crashin'*, you little idgit!"

"A DECIDEDLY *MINOR* CRASH," added Gax, "AS CRASHES GO."

Gax was being kind. Clearly we had done some very serious damage. Yellow steam was pouring out the front of the ship just beyond the windshield, and several red lights above the dashboard were flashing and buzzing.

"Aw, there goes the Twerbo-Fladiator coolant!" Spuckler gazed longingly at the yellow gases fading into the air. "I *knew* I shouldn'ta put that coolant tank in the nose of the ship."

"The Twerbo *what?*" I asked.

"The Twerbo-Fladiator coolant," replied Mr. Beeba. "It cools the Twerbo-Fladiator."

"And the Twerbo-Fladiator is . . ."

"A device for fladiating the twerb."

"Fladiating the twerb?"

He chuckled at my ignorance. "But of course, Akiko.

You can't expect a spaceship to go about with an unfla-diated twerb, now can you?"

I decided to leave it at that.

Spuckler ran to the back of the ship, pried open a door in the wall and pulled out a small piece of machinery that looked like a cross between a toaster oven and a Lava lamp. He was only able to pull it about three feet out of its compartment because it was held back by at least a half-dozen thick black-and-yellow cables.

"Won't be needin' *this* no more," Spuckler said as he severed one of the cables with a pair of clippers.

A small cloud of yellow gas—presumably the same stuff I'd just seen outside the windshield—billowed into the air, adding a nasty chemical odor to the already foul stench of grull.

Spuckler turned to me. "All right, 'Kiko. Looks like you got a job to do after all. I'm puttin' you in charge of coolin' the Twerbo-Fladiator."

I swallowed hard.

Spuckler pulled a lever, and a small seat unfolded from the wall. He had me sit down and strap myself in.

Then he lifted the toaster oven–Lava lamp and placed it in my lap.

"See this here dial?" He pointed to a small gauge on top of the contraption. Its needle quivered in a fan-shaped field that was shaded red on the far right edge.

"Every time this needle gets anywhere near the red part—*anywhere near it*—ya gotta do like this."

Spuckler lifted his left hand and placed it upright, slightly cupped, on the left side of his mouth. Then he lifted his *right* hand and placed *it* upright, slightly cupped, on the *right* side of his mouth, all the time gazing into my eyes to make sure I was paying the utmost attention. Then he lowered his face to the Lava lamp part of the machine and began blowing on it with all his might, as if he were trying to get a fire going on a camping trip.

*PHOOO-PHOOO-PHOOOOOOOO . . .*

Mr. Beeba, Gax, and Poog gathered around me, their faces indicating that I was being invested with a truly awesome responsibility.

"You mean . . . you want me to cool this thing down by . . . blowing on it . . . with my *mouth*," I said. "You're kidding, right?"

Spuckler's gaze grew even more intense. "I ain't never been so serious about nothin'. . . in my . . . entire . . . life."

All was silent except for a quietly buzzing light on the dashboard and the distant sound of another ship roaring past us outside. Looking around at everyone,

I realized that I, like it or not, was now the official Twerbo-Fladiator Cooler.

"Just one question, Spuckler," I said. "What happens if this thing overheats?"

Spuckler shot a glance at Gax, who shot a glance at Mr. Beeba, who shot a glance at Poog.

Spuckler looked at me with about as much intensity as his little eyes were capable of.

"You don't wanna know."

# Chapter 8

**Spuckler pushed buttons.** Spuckler pulled levers. Spuckler did everything he could to dislodge the front of our ship from the hole it had made in the stone. I held tightly to the Twerbo-Fladiator as we all lurched up and down and back and forth.

"Spuckler," said Mr. Beeba, "now that we're preparing to reenter the Labyrinth, I feel compelled to ask what I'm sure you'll agree is a highly pertinent question."

Spuckler grunted loudly as he pulled one more lever and finally managed to free the ship.

*GRR-JUNT!*

"Do you or do you not have even the *faintest* idea how to get through this maze?"

"I know this place like the backa my hand! It's left-right, left-left, right-right-right, left-right, left-left, right-right, left-left-left!"

For a moment there was no sound but the rumbling engines as we all took this in. Or tried to, anyway.

Then there was a very high-pitched series of warbly syllables: Poog, talking a good deal more loudly than he normally did, and for a lot longer than usual too.

"Poog says," translated Mr. Beeba, taking a deep breath before continuing, "that it's left-right, left-left, right-*left*-right, left-right, left-left, right-*left*, left-left-left."

There was another long pause. Spuckler shifted the ship into neutral and we just hovered there for a minute while he thought this over.

"Tha's what I *said!*" said Spuckler.

"Oh, but you said nothing of the kind, Spuckler. You claimed it was left-right, left-left, right-*right*-right, left-right—"

"Aw, fer cryin' out loud!" yelled Spuckler. "Poog! Get your purple heinie over here an' tell me which way t' go!"

Mr. Beeba and Poog took positions at the front of

the ship, flanking Spuckler like a pair of bodyguards. Every time we came to a fork in the gorge, Poog would chirp one of two different sounds, which Mr. Beeba would translate as either *left* or *right*. There was a bit of confusion at first (during which it occurred to me that maybe Spuckler didn't entirely know his left from his right to begin with), but eventually they had it down to a smoothly efficient system.

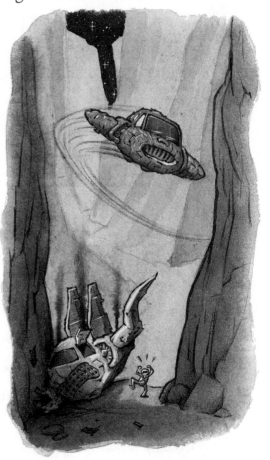

As we made our way through the maze, we began to see wreckage. At least three of the grand platinum ships that had started the race were now collapsed hunks of scrap metal on the roadside, their drivers beside them, gesturing angrily and stamping their feet in frustration. That left just eight ships—including ours—still in the race.

After another fifteen minutes and several more well-timed directions from Poog, we shot through one final narrow passageway and out into a spacious canyon. In the middle was an enormous loop of steel standing upright like a gigantic Hula-Hoop balanced on its side. It was covered with flashing lights and arrows pointing toward its center.

We soared through the hoop and up and away from the surface of Lulla-ma-Waygo.

*"Whaa-HOOOOOOH!"* cried Spuckler. "We did it!"

"You mean *Poog* did it," said Mr. Beeba.

"Yeah, all right," Spuckler said after a brief pause. "I reckon I owe ya one there, Poog."

Poog smiled modestly.

Within seconds we were back among the stars, sailing peacefully through the blackness. The Twerbo-Fladiator sat heavily in my lap. I watched the needle but it didn't seem to be moving much at all. Still, after all the fuss Spuckler had made about this new job of mine, I wasn't about to take my eye off that gauge.

Mr. Beeba and Gax continued shoveling grull into the belly of the ship, and before long the stars were racing by as fast as they ever had. Through the windshield I could see seven tiny slivers of light ahead in the distance: the other ships.

"More grull!" shouted Spuckler again and again. Each time, Mr. Beeba groaned and protested, but in the end he always grabbed his shovel and got to work. I could tell by the way he was digging deeper and deeper into the grull bin that we were already running low.

After a half hour or so Spuckler had relaxed to the point of sharing another of his strange space songs with us. This one he called "The Ballad of Ruggleby Kloink." There seemed to be an endless number of verses, one of which went something like this:

*"Where did he come from? No one knows,*

*With his fifteen eyes and his ten-foot nose,*

*Ya could smell him—hey!*
*From a mile awaaaaaaaaaay,*
*O, the girls did love ol' Ruggleby . . ."*

I was searching the room for something to stick in my ears when Spuckler mercifully ended his song to announce our next stop.

"There she is, folks!" he said, pointing at an irregularly shaped space station hovering before us. "Gorda Glassdok!"

# Chapter 9

**The nearer we got** to the ramshackle outpost, the stranger it looked. It was like a frontier town in one of those old Hollywood westerns, except instead of a desert it was surrounded by nothing but stars. There were several tall wooden towers and many more two- or three-story structures, all built around a central channel where spaceships could stop to refuel.

Mr. Beeba removed his spectacles. "Gorda Glassdok's owners boast that it is the universe's only wooden space station." He drew a handkerchief from his belt and wiped a speck from one of the lenses. "They are evidently somewhat less proud of its distinction as the universe's most abominable fire hazard. The entire complex has burned down more than one hundred and fifty times."

All seven of the other ships were drawn up alongside large spherical tanks, the only parts of the space station that were made of steel. Spuckler steered our ship toward a dingy wooden platform near the back: the grull depot.

"There ain't nothin' like Gorda Glassdok grull!" said Spuckler as he positioned the ship beneath a rickety wooden chute. "Ya can tell it's the good stuff 'cause it stinks so bad."

Gax and Spuckler hurried out to do some quick repairs while Mr. Beeba stayed inside to make sure the grull bin filled up properly. I got out to stretch my legs and have a look around.

Nearby was a small wooden kiosk run by a fat alien with big black eyes and very bad teeth. Every nook and cranny of his cramped quarters was packed with glass jars and crates full of oddly shaped vegetables, like an extraterrestrial farmers market. Strange reedy music was playing on a beat-up transistor radio dangling from the ceiling. He was tending a grill in front of him, slathering some sort of greasy sauce over a bunch of plump little things that looked like squids with insect wings.

60

As I drew closer, he snatched up one of them with his bare hands, thrust a wooden skewer through it, and jabbed it in my direction.

"*Horb-nok?*" he asked with a big gap-toothed smile. "*Ob-zwotch horb-nok. Ob-zwotch, OB-ZWOTCH!*"

"Uh, no thanks," I said before walking away as quickly as I could. "I already ate."

I went over to the front of our ship, where Spuckler and Gax were busily fixing the damage we'd done on

Lulla-ma-Waygo. Just then a voice echoed from somewhere up above.

"Still using grull, eh, Boach?" There was a dismissive snort. "I respect that. Very *old school* of you."

Gax's head spun all the way around.

"Bluggamin Streed," said Spuckler without taking his eyes from his work. "Had a feelin' I'd be runnin' into you on this race."

I looked up. A tall man gazed down at us from several stories above. He was very young—maybe even still a teenager—and dressed in a spotless white spacesuit. His hair was blond, his skin darkly tanned.

"You made it through Lulla-ma-Waygo in *this* hunka junk?" the man said. "You lead a charmed life, my friend."

"*Boach's Bullet* ain't never failed me yet, Bluggy," said Spuckler, still keeping his eyes on the repair work. "An' I'll take grull over that highfalutin brew *you're* usin' any day of the week."

"Thermo-Propahol wins races, Boach," said Streed. "Left you in the dust in the Whundy 2000, as I recall."

"Ain't you got nothin' *better* to do, Bluggy?"

Spuckler finally met Streed's gaze.

"Oh, I'm sorry, Mr. Boach," said Streed with exaggerated politeness. He turned and disappeared over the edge of the platform. "Still kind of sore about that, aren't you?"

"Dagnabbed upstart," grumbled Spuckler as he soldered a piece of steel back into place. "Sassy as they come."

I was going to ask Spuckler to tell me more about

Bluggamin Streed, but I got the feeling he wasn't exactly in the mood to talk right then.

*GUDDA-GUDDA-GUDDA-GUDDA-GUDDA . . .*

A thunderous rumble filled the air as grull poured through the chute into our ship. Five minutes later the noise died down, then came to a stop altogether. Mr. Beeba's head popped out of the door of the ship, his hair green with grull dust.

"Full to the gills!" he announced.

"All righty," said Spuckler with one final blast of his soldering gun. "Let's get goin'."

A minute or two later we were all back in our assigned places, and the wooden way station of Gorda Glassdok was far behind us. As the stars whizzed past, Spuckler reached down to a grease-stained paper bag he had brought in with him before we took off.

"Got a surprise for ya, 'Kiko," he said as he opened the bag, pulled out one of the blackened squid creatures, and slapped it into my hand. It was still smoking from the grill. "A barbecued horb-nok. Think of it as a li'l reward for comin' along with us!"

I smiled what I hoped was a convincing smile.

"Thanks, Spuckler."

"Don't mention it." He took a big chomp out of a horb-nok he'd bought for himself. "You keep that Twerbo-Fladiator cool and I'll see if I can rustle up another one for ya."

Spuckler polished off his snack in just a few bites, then began calling out for more grull.

"Come on, now, Beebs! We gotta really get cookin' if we're gonna keep ahead of"—a split-second pause—"all them ships back there!" Spuckler grunted, pulling levers on the dashboard left, right, and center.

All them ships? Or just one ship in particular? Spuckler was too proud to say it, I guess, but I knew what was on his mind. From now on this race had nothing to do with winning the Centauri Cup, and everything to do with crossing the finish line before Bluggamin Streed.

# Chapter 10

**We entered a long stretch** of the race in which there was nothing to do but fly straight on to the next big hurdle. Spuckler had Mr. Beeba madly shoveling grull into the ship's belly every ten minutes, eventually bringing us back to second place: one ship ahead of us, six ships—one of them Bluggamin Streed's—far behind. Gax kept a watchful eye on a series of dials and gauges throughout the ship, rolling from one to the other on his squeaky wheels. Poog stayed up near the front of the ship with Spuckler, and I sat strapped in my seat, occasionally cupping my hands and blowing on the Twerbo-Fladiator. The needle didn't look like it was getting any nearer to the red part of the gauge, but I blew on the thing anyway, just in case.

We all settled into the rhythm of our own routines, and the rumbling of the wall behind my back was starting to make me feel awfully sleepy. I checked my watch again: 2 P.M. If I were still on Earth, I'd have already been back from Middleton Park for several hours, two or three big bowls of my mom's vegetable soup in my belly, curled up on the couch with a blanket and a book, nothing but my heavy eyelids to keep me from drifting off to . . .

*DREEEE-YAA! DREEEE-YAA! DREEEEEEEE-YAAA!*

What a screech! Mr. Beeba dropped to his knees. Gax spun around. Spuckler leaped from his seat.

There in front of us on the floor was . . .

. . . well, it looked like a *bug*. One of those little roly-poly gray ones that curl up into a ball when you touch them. But bigger. A *lot* bigger. It was about the size of a soccer ball, and it was shaped like one too, all closed up and rocking back and forth on the floor. It was covered with bluish gray scales, tinged green from grull dust.

"Don't touch it!" Mr. Beeba said, holding his shovel above his head like a club.

"Wh-what is it?" I asked, peering over the Twerbo-Fladiator at the strange gray creature.

Spuckler drew a red laser pistol from a holster at his side. "I'll tell ya what it is," he said. "It's a stowaway."

Poog floated in to get a closer look. Gax scooted over to Spuckler's side.

"HOW DID IT GET INSIDE THE SHIP, SIR?" he asked. "DO YOU THINK IT'S BEEN HERE ALL ALONG?"

"It was hidin' in the grull we took on at Gorda Glassdok." Spuckler aimed his laser pistol squarely at the little gray ball. "Beeba must've tossed the li'l sucker in the fire. Tha's what all that yappin' was about."

Just then the little ball opened up, just a crack, and two tiny blue antennae emerged from inside. There were little purple bulbs on the ends, as if they'd grown from inside some strange alien flower.

"Shoot it, Spuckler!" Mr. Beeba squealed. "Now, before it attacks us!"

"No, wait!" I said.

"Wait?" Mr. Beeba's eyes were as big as baseballs. "Wait until it attaches itself to my forehead, liquefies my brain, and slurps it out like a smagberry milk shake? No, no, no, Akiko. Now is not the time for waiting. Now is the time for aiming and zapping!"

"Look," I said, "we've got to think this through. Who knows if this creature is good or bad or, or . . . neither? We can't just zap it without asking any questions."

"Sure we can, 'Kiko," said Spuckler. "I do it all th' time. Askin' questions is for sissies."

The creature's blue antennae touched the floor in several places and twirled slowly in the air like a pair of rubber periscopes. Then they silently withdrew into the center of the ball, which curled itself back up as tightly as before.

I guess I should have been afraid of the thing. I mean, I've seen those movies where aliens are all scary and slimy and do horrible things to people. But this creature was nothing like that. It reminded me of a frightened puppy.

"All right, on the counta three," said Spuckler, stepping forward and extending his laser pistol to near-point-blank range. "One . . ."

"No, Spuckler!" I said. "I won't let you hurt it! This creature hasn't done us any harm. Maybe it stowed away on this ship by accident!"

Spuckler squinted at me like he thought I was nuts. He stopped counting, though, and pulled his pistol back a bit.

I carefully set the Twerbo-Fladiator on the floor and unbuckled my seat belt.

"Akiko!" Mr. Beeba said, his voice trembling with tension. "What are you doing?"

"Shhhhhh."

Everyone got very, very quiet. I dropped down on my hands and knees and crawled forward until I was only about a foot or two from the creature.

"Don't be afraid," I said, just a breath above a whisper. "We won't hurt you."

With that the little ball opened up again and the antennae reemerged. This time they stretched toward me and moved in slow, silent circles, as if studying my face.

"Come on," I said. "Open up a little more. Let us see what you look like."

The little antennae reached out until they were just a

few inches from my face, each positioned neatly before one of my cheeks.

Mr. Beeba swallowed loudly.

The antennae quietly withdrew again into the little gray ball, and then, ever so slowly, the creature uncurled itself. The hard exterior folded back to reveal puffy pink flesh within. One by one, soft little legs popped out, until there were six in all. They extended from either side of the creature's body, which was as plump as a newborn piglet. The stalks of the blue antennae receded into a hole where the neck should have been; for a second or two I thought the creature had no head! But then the hole opened wider and wider, and, like some kind of alien turtle, out came a round blue face with big, blinking, shiny black eyes and a tiny toothless mouth. All in all, it was the most harmless little thing you could imagine.

"Hmf!" snorted Spuckler, clearly disappointed.

"Mr. Beeba," I asked without taking my eyes from the creature, "have you ever seen one of these before?"

"Never," he replied. "He looks like a rather kindly little fellow, though, doesn't he?"

The creature smiled a big toothless smile and nodded.

"He understands what we're saying!" I said.

"You mustn't jump to conclusions, Akiko," Mr. Beeba warned. "In my experience aliens of this sort hardly *ever* possess the faculties of speech recognition—"

"Ozlips."

There was shocked silence. The creature had just spoken to us. He turned his little face from Mr. Beeba and me to Spuckler, Gax, and Poog, smiling and nodding meekly.

"Ozlips," he said again, his voice husky, like a child with a cold.

"Ozlips?" I asked.

"Ozlips," the creature said again. "Moy neem. Ozlips."

"Moy nin," said Mr. Beeba. "I believe he's speaking a dialect of the G'niki tongue. . . ."

"Nu, nu!" said the creature, frowning at Mr. Beeba. "Moy *neem*. Moy *neem* esh Ozlips."

"Moy *neen*, eh?" Mr. Beeba rubbed his jaw. "It's

Pradasha. I'm sure of it. An exceptionally rare language spoken only on the planet Triddi B'Doosh. . . ."

"Nu-nu-nu-nu-nu." The creature waved his little arms in frustration. "Moy *neem* esh Ozlips."

"*Neem?*" Mr. Beeba repeated, now looking thoroughly baffled. "Neem! I'm pretty sure that's the Droobanese word for *postage overdue.* . . ."

"Mr. Beeba," I said, "I think what he's trying to say is 'My *name* . . . is Ozlips.'"

"Yish, yish, yish," said the creature, nodding enthusiastically. "Moy *neem!* Moy neem esh Ozlips!"

"Heavens!" was all Mr. Beeba could say. "His pronunciation is *atrocious.*"

"Hello, Ozlips," I said, smiling. "Nice to meet you. My name is Akiko."

"Gah-gi-go," said Ozlips, smiling back at me. "Nesh tu beet chu."

"Did you hear that? He said 'Nice to meet you'!"

"All right, all right." Spuckler stuffed his laser pistol back in its holster. "So he can talk a little. He's still a sneaky little stowaway. We'll toss him off the ship first chance we get."

"Spuckler!" I said, raising my voice. "We can't abandon him in the middle of nowhere. Maybe he was hiding in the grull for a *reason*."

Ozlips waddled over a little closer to me.

"Yish, yish!" he said. "Reeshun, reeshun. Perry *kood* reeshun!"

Spuckler squinted again.

"Moy mashtur," Ozlips continued, raising his stubby little arms to his head and scrunching up his eyes in a show of pain. "Moy mashtur peet-mi. Heff-ry dee peet-mi. Peet-mi, peet-mi, peet-mi!"

Everyone turned to me, clearly not having understood a word. Suddenly *I* was the expert on translating Ozlips-ese.

"Didn't you hear him? He says his master . . . beat him."

There was an awed silence.

"What about the 'heff-ry dee' part?" Mr. Beeba asked.

"Simple: 'Every day.'"

"Oh dear," Mr. Beeba said. "An abused servant. Poor little chap, no *wonder* he wanted to escape Gorda Glassdok."

"Hey, now, this ain't no charity ship!" said Spuckler. "A stowaway's a stowaway, plain an' simple. We gotta get rid of 'im!"

"No, Spuckler." I put a protective arm around Ozlips. "So long as I'm on this ship, he's staying right here."

"'Kiko," Spuckler whined, "we're tryin' t' win a *race* here. I don't want this little alien twerp slowin' us down."

"He's not a twerp," I said, glaring at Spuckler. "And he's *not* going to slow us down. Who knows, he might even be able to help us win."

"Yish!" Ozlips said. He nodded excitedly and moved even closer to my side. "*Hail*-pew! *Hail*-pew!"

"Come on, Spuckler," I said. "Look at him. He's *cute*."

Spuckler stared at me—at the *two* of us, really—his eyes squinted nearly shut, his lips like stone.

"Cute," he mumbled. "I *hate* cute."

No sooner had these words left his lips than the whole ship rocked violently to one side, sending all of us tumbling to the floor. I threw my arms around Ozlips, forgetting all about the Twerbo-Fladiator.

Just as suddenly the ship was nice and steady again. Through the windshield we saw a fiery flash and a big white rocket zooming ahead of us.

"Streed!" Spuckler growled as he leaped back to the controls.

# Chapter 11

**Spuckler cried out** for grull, but Mr. Beeba was already on the job, heaving shovelfuls into the ship's furnace as fast as his spindly arms would allow. I strapped myself back into my seat and held both the Twerbo-Fladiator and Ozlips tightly, one under each arm.

"He bumped us," Spuckler kept saying, over and over. "*Bumped* us! I can't believe it!"

I noticed with a quiet horror that there was a tiny crack in the Lava lamp part of the Twerbo-Fladiator. Had that happened a second ago? Maybe it had been there before and I hadn't seen it.

Yeah, *right*. I decided not to say anything.

*GUDDA-GUDDA-GUDDA-GUDDA . . .*

Mr. Beeba's grull shoveling was paying off. We passed a silver ship—the one that had been in first place just minutes before—and drew closer to Streed.

"HE'S DOING THIS ON PURPOSE, SIR," Gax warned, "TRYING TO PREEMPTIVELY EXHAUST OUR FUEL SUPPLY."

"I know that, Gax," Spuckler replied with irritation. "Whaddaya think I am, some kinda nitwit?"

Gax wisely chose not to answer this question.

"BUT HADN'T WE BETTER CONSERVE OUR GRULL FOR LATER IN THE RACE?"

"Yeah, of *course* we should . . . ," said Spuckler, "but he *bumped* us, Gax! I can't let 'im get away with that!"

Every time we got to a point where we were nearly neck and neck with Streed, he'd accelerate even more and leave us shuddering in his wake.

"The little ding-danged frim-frammin' varmint!" Spuckler grumbled, sounding like there were other words—really *ugly* ones—that he'd rather use just then.

By now the needle on the Twerbo-Fladiator was moving toward the red zone on a regular basis. I cupped my hands and blew on it with all my might, finding to my relief that two or three strong puffs were enough to cool it down each time.

Ozlips, seeing what I was doing, tried to help out. His tiny little breaths were more or less useless; judging from the size of his body, he only had lungs the size of lima beans! Still, I was touched to see how hard he was working on my behalf.

"Thanks, Ozlips," I said.

"Moy plissure!" he replied with a gasp, already thoroughly winded.

Poog began making warbly little announcements

about once every five minutes. Mr. Beeba, consumed with his shoveling duties, failed to translate any of it.

"Hey, come on," I said at last. "What's Poog saying?"

"He's simply keeping us informed," Mr. Beeba wheezed, propping himself unsteadily on the handle of his shovel, "of our progress toward the Almost-Black Hole of Luzbert-7."

"The *Almost*-Black Hole?"

"It's more of a deep shade of indigo," Mr. Beeba explained with a grunt, already back at work.

I took a few seconds to think this one over. Mrs. Jackson, my science teacher back at Middleton Elementary, had once spent an entire lesson teaching us about black holes. I was really hungry that day and wasn't paying as much attention as I should have. But I did remember at least a *few* things.

"Now wait a minute," I said to Mr. Beeba. "A black hole can't be indigo. Or *any* color, can it? It's not even really a hole. It's like a tiny little spot in space where gravity sucks everything in, right? I'm pretty sure that's what my teacher told us, anyway."

"Let me guess," Mr. Beeba replied. "You were told that it is a point of extreme mass in space-time with a gravitational field so intense that it traps all electromagnetic radiation, including light."

"Um," I said, "*some*thing like that, yeah."

"Ah, Earth scientists," Mr. Beeba said with a chuckle. "So much left to learn!"

I was going to ask another question when I felt a mild vibration against my left arm, like the gentle purring of a kitten: Ozlips. He had fallen asleep—from the exhaustion of trying to cool the Twerbo-Fladiator, I guess—and was curled up against me, very nearly as small and round as when we'd first seen him.

"Really!" I whispered. "How could they even *think* of abandoning this poor little guy?"

He wormed around a little, burrowing himself even deeper into the warmth of my arm.

"More grull!" Spuckler shouted for the umpteenth time.

We were now within a quarter mile or so of Streed's ship and were gaining on him bit by bit. Looming ahead of us was a huge mass of blue clouds spiraling in toward a . . .

. . . well, it was a dark blue hole. But not dark blue, really.

It was a deep shade of indigo.

# Chapter 12

**"We gotta get in there** b'fore Streed!" Spuckler shouted, pulling down every lever on the entire dashboard. "The racin' order's pretty much set once everyone goes through the Hole! It's pretty near impossible to make up lost ground later on."

I held on tightly to Ozlips as I watched our progress through the windshield. With each passing second we drew closer to Streed's ship. The spiraling blue edge of the Almost-Black Hole spread out above and below us. We began to experience turbulence that quickly grew so violent, I thought the ship was going to shatter into a million pieces.

"WE'VE GOT TO KILL THE ENGINE, SIR!" Gax cried. "NO ONE FLIES INTO THE HOLE FULL THROTTLE LIKE THIS!"

"No one but me, Gax!" Spuckler said, his voice all but submerged in the rattling of the ship and the high-pitched howl of the engine.

"Spuckler!" Mr. Beeba wailed as he tossed the grull shovel to the floor and strapped himself into his seat. "Shut off the engine at once, you lunatic! This will be the death of us all!"

Again we were nearly neck and neck with Streed. With all the shaking and rocking it was hard to see who was ahead. The whirling indigo clouds of the Almost-Black Hole were now surrounding us on all sides. Directly in front of us was the hole itself: slightly oval, shimmering and flashing with bursts of blue electricity.

"Hang on to yer hats, folks!" Spuckler shouted as he pulled a big black knob from the dashboard, finally killing the engine. The rattling immediately subsided and the scream of the engine slowly died down to a low-pitched hum.

I breathed a sigh of relief, thinking the worst was over. (Yeah, I know. How stupid can you get?)

Looking around, I noticed with some alarm that Mr. Beeba and Spuckler were gritting their teeth and closing their eyes. Gax scooted over and locked himself into his spot on the floor, while Poog floated toward me and Ozlips, a worried expression on his face.

The gravitational force of the Almost-Black Hole took over. Spuckler had let go of the steering wheel entirely and was holding on to the dashboard with tensed, outstretched arms. Through one of the portals I could see Streed's ship: It was just a dozen yards or so away from us, and it was whirling around so quickly, it looked like a spinning top!

That's when our ship gradually turned upside down. We flipped over once. Then twice. Then a third time and a fourth, until finally we were spinning repeatedly, faster and faster, flattened against the walls, getting whipped around and around like socks in a clothes dryer. Finally I just had to close my eyes because everything was turning into a twirling, circular blur.

*SHUDDA*
*SHUDDA*
*SHUDDA*
The ship was filled with this weird rhythmic sound, loud and deep, pulsing through the walls and into our bodies. Then—
*ZZZZZRRRRRR*

and

*FFLLRRRRRRRRR*
and
*SPPLLLLLUUUUURRRRRRRRRPP!*

I opened my eyes.

The spinning had stopped. The ship was perfectly level again.

Okay. You know what it's like when you're spinning around and around and then you suddenly stop: You get dizzy. Well, I was dizzy all right. More than dizzy. Way, way, *WAY* more than dizzy. I was so disoriented right then, I'd have had better luck walking on my hands than my feet. Even sitting down, with seat belts strapping me in, I could *still* barely keep my balance. So I just held tightly to the Twerbo-Fladiator and waited for the tornado in my head to spin itself out.

The ship might have stopped flipping, but our speed hadn't been reduced at all. Now we were flying faster than ever, even with the engine shut off, zooming through space so quickly, the stars in the windows were nothing more than stretched-out streaks of light.

"That's it," I heard Spuckler say. "We're on the other side."

The fixtures of the ship were still whirling wildly in my eyes, but little by little I was able to focus on individual objects. Then—it took a while, for some reason—I became aware of a slimy feeling on my arms and face. Looking down, I saw that I was covered from head to toe with some sort of weird yellow goop. And I wasn't the only one. Mr. Beeba, Spuckler, Gax, Poog, every last square inch of the interior of the ship . . . everyone and everything was just dripping with this awful greasy gooey stuff. It gave off a really nasty smell, too, like old cheese—you know, the kind of cheese that's pretty stinky even when it's *not* old.

"Black-hole mucus," said Mr. Beeba, wiping a dollop of the stuff from his eyes. "One of the unfortunate side effects of passing through a black hole."

Ugh! It was without a doubt the grossest substance in the universe.

"My science teacher definitely didn't tell us about *this*."

Gax had found some kind of vacuum-cleaner thing inside his body and was using it to suck the goop off Poog before attending to himself. The rest of us tried to clean ourselves off, but it was pretty much a losing battle. The yellow goo was so oily that even hot water and industrial-strength detergent probably wouldn't have done much. Even Gax's vacuum cleaner was only partially effective, leaving him and Poog still half-covered with the stuff. Spuckler was the only one who didn't seem to mind how filthy he'd become. He was too busy revving the engine back up to full throttle and scanning the windshield for signs of Bluggamin Streed. He was practically bouncing with glee.

"I think we musta passed him back there in the hole! I can't see him round here nowhere!"

Incredible. We were now in first place. Maybe we'd win this race after all.

Just then I noticed with a shock that I was still holding the Twerbo-Fladiator, but not . . .

"Ozlips!" I cried. "Where is he? I've lost him!"

He had utterly disappeared.

Mr. Beeba stared at me and chuckled. Spuckler turned around, looked at me, and broke into loud hyena-like laughter. Even Poog was smiling.

"What?" I asked. *"What?"*

Mr. Beeba smiled apologetically.

"He's on top of your head, Akiko," he said.

Sure enough, Ozlips had somehow climbed up on my head and was—believe it or not—*licking* my hair.

Mr. Beeba stepped closer to me and examined Ozlips with great interest.

"Good heavens," he half whispered. "Ozlips is giving you a jolly good cleaning."

"He is?"

"My word, yes," he answered, stepping around to view me from a variety of angles. "He's licking that mucus off you as if it were a right tasty little treat."

Ozlips didn't stop at the top of my head. He was just getting started.

In a matter of seconds he had worked his way down to my face. I wish you could know what it feels like to have that silky little tongue flicking across your cheeks. It was like being kissed by an extremely affectionate fish. Let's just say it's a good thing I'm not particularly ticklish.

Before long Ozlips had removed every last trace of the black-hole mucus from my arms and hands and neck and all my clothes, including the bottoms of my shoes! He sucked the mucus off the tips of my shoelaces and licked his lips as if he'd just finished off a plate of spaghetti.

But he still wasn't done.

He moved right on to Mr. Beeba and started all over again. Unfortunately Mr. Beeba was ticklish—*extremely* ticklish—and for several minutes the ship echoed with the sound of his cackling laughter, interrupted only by desperate pleas to "Stop!" and "Take it easy, you little fiend!" Now it was *my* turn to smile.

In the space of half an hour Ozlips cleaned the black-hole mucus off Mr. Beeba, Spuckler, Gax, Poog, the floor, the ceiling, and all the walls of the whole ship. How he managed to fit all that stuff into his tiny little belly is something I will never understand (and a subject that Mr. Beeba will no doubt theorize about for the rest of his life).

His goo feast finished, Ozlips crawled again into the

crook of my arm. Then he tossed his head back and let out a loud and impossibly long belch.

"Nnnn," he said. "De-*litz*-zusss."

A few seconds later he was sound asleep again.

After that everyone began to treat Ozlips a little better than they had before. He became a mascot for us, like a stray dog we'd picked up and decided to call our own. Even Spuckler seemed to be getting used to him.

"I guess he ain't all that bad," he said, "for a stow-away."

# Chapter 13

**There was only** one more stop before the last stretch of the race. Actually, I don't think you could call it a stop. It was kind of a *rolling* stop.

Spuckler used a walkie-talkie thing on the dashboard to make a quick call, something about "two tons" and "an extra twen'y gilpots if ya make it snappy."

A moment later I saw a large rectangular spacecraft zooming in toward us from up ahead. It was like a big shoe box with one wide groove cut in the bottom. There were small windows on the sides through which I saw the shapes of—well, there's no other way to say it: little green men.

"Fuelers," Spuckler explained. "They got a lock on the market with this race. If you wanna get refueled without stoppin', they're the only choice ya got."

The shoe-box ship, which was about four or five times larger than our own, carefully adjusted its speed and glided over us until we were enclosed. Spuckler punched a few buttons and barked more orders into his walkie-talkie. There were a bang, a clang, and several loud thunks before I heard—and smelled—fresh grull pouring into our ship from above.

*GUDDA-GUDDA-GUDDA-GUDDA-GUDDA . . .*

The grull bin was about half full when I saw Streed's ship pull in next to ours. He rolled down a window at the front of the ship—almost like a car at a fast-food drive-through—and signaled for Spuckler to do the same. Spuckler groaned but flicked a switch that opened a large window in the right-hand wall of our ship.

There, no more than fifty feet away from us, was Bluggamin Streed, grinning and resting a white-clothed elbow on the ledge of his window.

"The Hole spat you through faster than me, old-timer." His sun-tanned face was smiling but angry. "You're a lucky man."

"It's called *skill*, Bluggy." Spuckler leaned back in his chair. "Watch me. Ya might learn somethin'."

"Don't get sassy, Spuck." Streed pointed a threatening finger. "That Hole was a demon today. Three ships got so mucked up, they're out of the race."

Three more gone? That left just five ships, including ours!

"Th' Hole knows better'n to mess with *me*," said Spuckler, giving me a wink. He looked a little tired.

"Mark my words, Spuck. The Centauri Cup is mine."

Spuckler gritted his teeth. "We'll see about that."

"*See* about that?" Streed's laughter echoed off the walls, surprisingly loud. "The only thing *you're* going to see is the tail end of my ship, crossing the finish line before you do."

Spuckler yanked a knob . . .

*K'CHOK!*

. . . slamming the
window shut. Grull was
still pouring into the ship,
but he was already pushing
buttons, revving the engine.

"THERE'S STILL MORE COMING,
SIR," protested Gax. "WE'VE ONLY
RECEIVED THREE-QUARTERS OF THE
LOAD."

"Times a-wastin', Gax." Spuckler snapped a lever
down and the ship rocked and shuddered.

"BUT—"

*BBBRRRRRRRUUUUUUUUUMMMMMMM!*

*Boach's Bullet* tore out of the refueling ship like a race-
horse bursting from a starting gate. Through a window
in the rear of the ship I saw a trail of grull spiraling
through space behind us.

I was alarmed by Spuckler's behavior, but also glad
that we were still in first place. So long as we could stay
ahead of Streed . . .

"HE'S DONE REFUELING, SIR," Gax announced, "AND

GAINING ON US! WE'RE NO MORE THAN A MILE AHEAD
OF HIM AT BEST."

"*Grull!*"

We all jumped back to our duties. Mr. Beeba shoveled grull into the ship's furnace more frantically than
ever, and I huffed and puffed on the Twerbo-Fladiator,
which definitely seemed to be overheating with increasing regularity. There was no problem cooling it down,
but I really had to keep an eye on it.

"THREE-QUARTERS OF A MILE, SIR!" said Gax.

"The dagnabbed little runt," Spuckler growled,
throwing switches and punching buttons. "He jus' don't
know when to quit!"

Finally the grull delivered the speed we needed.

"HOLDING STEADY AT THREE-QUARTERS OF A MILE,
SIR!" said Gax.

I breathed a sigh of relief. For the time being, at
least, it looked like we'd be able to maintain our slim
lead. I asked Mr. Beeba if there were any more hurdles
left.

"Just one," he answered. "The Jaws of McVluddapuck."

"*Jaws?*" I asked. "That doesn't sound good."

"It isn't," he replied. "The Jaws of McVluddapuck are the remains of a planet—the *planet* McVludda-puck—that was cleaved neatly in half many eons ago by an enormous blade of solar radiation." He paused to shovel another load of grull into the furnace. Gasping for breath, he continued. "Since then the two halves of McVluddapuck have been slamming together with uncanny precision once every 7.3 seconds."

He gave me a moment to form a picture of this in my mind.

"There's a sort of balletic grace to it, really. Aesthetically speaking, I'm sure we'd all enjoy it if not for the fact that we'll be trying to fly this ship between the two halves before they smash together again."

I sat there blinking.

"Try not to worry, Akiko," Mr. Beeba added. "Spuckler's been practicing. He's made it through the Jaws in well under 7.1 seconds. Haven't you, Spuckler?"

When the confident reply didn't come, we both turned and saw to our horror that Spuckler was slumped over in the driver's seat, asleep at the wheel.

"Spuckler!" I set Ozlips and the Twerbo-Fladiator on the floor and ran to the front of the ship. Mr. Beeba got there first and began checking Spuckler's pulse. Gax and Poog, who had been busy keeping an eye on Streed's ship, raced over and joined us at Spuckler's side.

I gave Spuckler a good shake and he slowly came to.

"I'm awright, I'm awright," he said. He was anything *but* all right. He looked like he was struggling just to keep his eyes open.

"Strange," said Mr. Beeba. "His heart rate is fine, but he's clearly in need of rest."

Poog frowned. He looked very troubled.

"I'm awright, I said!" Spuckler insisted. "Git back t' yer stations. We got a race t' win here."

"This is really weird," I whispered to Gax. "Have you ever seen him like this before?"

"NEVER, MA'AM," Gax answered. "SOMETHING'S DEFINITELY HAD AN

ADVERSE EFFECT ON HIM. THE PASSAGE THROUGH THE ALMOST-BLACK HOLE, PERHAPS . . ."

The whole ship rocked to one side as Streed's ship moved into position alongside us. We were still ahead of him, but just barely.

"Streed!" Spuckler cried. "'Kiko, I'm gonna need your help."

"H-help?"

"I'm havin' trouble seein' straight," he whispered.

"Spuckler," said Mr. Beeba, "you're in no shape to fly this ship. You need rest!"

"Back to the shovel, ya lazy varmint," Spuckler said. "We're losin' steam!"

Mr. Beeba stepped back uncertainly.

"Go on!" Spuckler barked. "Snap to it!"

Mr. Beeba reluctantly went back to his duties.

"Gax, see whatcha can do about coolin' the Fladiator," said Spuckler. "I'm gonna need 'Kiko up here with me from now on."

"YES, SIR," said Gax as he wheeled himself over to Ozlips and the Twerbo-Fladiator. He began using a little hair dryer–shaped tool to perform my earlier duties.

"Poog," said Spuckler, "keep an eye on ol' Streed over there. Let me know if he's fixin' to bump us again."

Poog, still frowning, floated over to the portal with the best view of Streed's ship, leaving Spuckler and me alone.

"Okay, 'Kiko," Spuckler said, "jus' b'tween you an' me, I don't feel so hot."

"I can see that."

"So I'm gonna show ya how to fly this ship."

"*Me?* Are you nuts?" My knees turned to jelly. "I'm just a *kid*. I'm still working on my *bike*-riding skills!"

Spuckler remained silent for a moment, his eyes very sad and serious.

"You sayin' ya ain't gonna help me, 'Kiko?" he asked. "You're gonna quit on me? Right now, when I really *need*ja?"

"I didn't say that, Spuckler. But . . ."

"But what?"

There was another long pause. I looked around at the others, everyone doing his best to keep the ship flying its fastest. Through one of the portals I could see the nose of Streed's ship, edging its way past us by what looked like a matter of inches.

"I'm going to need a pad of paper," I said. "I'll *never* remember all this stuff if I don't write it down."

# Chapter 14

**Learning to fly** *Boach's Bullet* was just about the most difficult thing I've ever had to do in my life. There were knobs to pull, dials to turn, and levers to switch up and down. My head was swimming with all Spuckler's directions:

"This one regulates th' honk-oddle pressure."

"This baby keeps the Rimpley pistons from knockin' into one another."

"I forget what this one does, but ya better give 'er a good tug once in a while jus' t' be safe."

I scribbled down page after page of notes, drawing crude little pictures to remind myself of what I had to do and how to do it and how often.

"Not bad, 'Kiko. You're gettin' the hang of it."

Spuckler did his best to appear energetic, but I could tell he was suffering. Beads of sweat covered his forehead and his eyes had this very faraway look, like he was wearing himself out just standing there.

"Spuckler, you need rest," I said. "Why don't you go lie down for a minute?"

"I'm fine, 'Kiko, I'm fine," he insisted, rubbing his eyes.

Then, not more than half a minute later: "Ya know, 'Kiko, you're right. Lyin' down for a minute or two would do me a worlda good right now."

I swallowed hard. Was I ready for this? Not by a long shot.

"I'll be back in a jiff, 'Kiko," Spuckler said, raising his finger to make one last point. "Don't worry about Streed. Don't even think about him. It don't matter if we win or lose. Just do your best."

Spuckler's eyes were half closed. His hair was black with sweat.

"Go lie down, Spuckler," I said, wishing he wouldn't.

"Thank ya, 'Kiko."

Then it was just me flying the ship.

I raised my head and looked through the windshield at the boundless black sea of stars beyond. Had I really just agreed to take over flying the ship for Spuckler? What was I *thinking*?

"More grull, Akiko?" I heard Mr. Beeba ask from behind me. He evidently had no problem accepting a fifth grader as his captain.

"Um, yeah," I said, shooting a glance through the window at Streed's ship, now a good yard or two ahead of us.

I looked at the dashboard with all its knobs and dials and flashing orange buttons. It was like sitting in the cockpit of an airplane, I swear, but with more switches and more lights. There were five or six levers for acceleration alone, each one for making the ship move forward in a different way. I consulted my notes and pulled one on the far right of the dashboard, one that I thought Spuckler had said was for increasing acceleration gradually.

Oops.

*DROGG-DROGG-DROGG-DROGG-DROGG*

The whole ship shuddered and shook, tipping over until it was nearly upside down.

*KLANG!*

*"Yyyyooooowch!"*

(I have no idea what made the first sound, but I'm pretty sure the second one was Mr. Beeba.)

"Sorry!" I said.

I took the lever I'd just pulled and *un*-pulled it as quickly as I could. The ship went back to flying straight again, but now Streed was ten or twenty yards ahead of us.

I couldn't bear to let him beat us. Even if it was okay with Spuckler, it wasn't okay with me.

I tried lever after lever, knob after knob, and after shutting the lights off and on and cranking up a strange alien radio station to full blast, I had to admit to myself that I really didn't have the faintest idea how to fly this ship.

"Mr. Beeba!" I shouted.

"More grull?" he asked.

"Forget about the grull! Get up here and help me out for a second!"

A moment later Mr. Beeba was at my side, looking around as if it was the first time he'd ever been so close to the controls of the ship. Or *any* ship, for that matter.

"Heavens!" he said. "So many flashing lights! That red one's pretty. What does it do?"

"I was going to ask you if you knew how to fly this ship," I said, "but I think you already answered my question."

"No need to get snippy about it, Akiko."

We both turned to Gax, who together with Ozlips was going to great lengths to keep the Twerbo-Fladiator cool.

"Gax, old boy," said Mr. Beeba, "you don't happen to know how to fly this ship, do you?"

"INTERSTELLAR REGULATIONS HAVE BANNED ROBOTS FROM LEARNING HOW TO FLY ANY AND ALL SPACESHIPS, SIR," Gax replied, "EVER SINCE AN ANDROID CRASHED ONE OF THOSE BIG GALACTIC CRUISERS BACK IN '29."

"Poog?"

Poog slowly shook his head back and forth. I couldn't tell if he meant "No, I don't know how to fly this ship" or "No, you've got to do this on your own."

I was running out of people to turn to.

Wait!

"Ozlips?"

Ozlips shook his head and made a gesture of helplessness with his stubby little arms, as if to show that he couldn't even pull down a single lever, much less help me fly the ship.

I gazed through the windshield as Streed's ship pulled farther and farther ahead of us.

"I'll go wake up Spuckler," said Mr. Beeba.

"No. Wait," I said.

Spuckler was flat on his back on a narrow bed he'd folded out from the wall. He was sound asleep and snoring loudly.

"Let him rest," I said, a little surprised by the words coming out of my mouth. "*I'm* going to fly this ship. Spuckler showed me how. He's counting on me . . . and I'm going to do it."

"Y-you are?" Mr. Beeba asked. "How?"

"Trial and error."

"Akiko, with all due respect—"

"More grull!" I shouted, sounding about as much like Spuckler as I probably ever will. "Everyone back to your stations!"

I tightened my safety belts until it felt like the driver's seat was permanently glued to my back. I trained my eyes on Streed's ship, now miles and miles ahead of us. It was now or never.

"Hold on tight, everyone," I called out. "This is *not* going to be a smooth ride."

# Chapter 15

## FL-FL-FLAAAAAAAAAAMMMM!

I was pulling levers, pressing buttons, yanking knobs. I was throwing switches, twirling dials, stamping on pedals. I'd chucked out my notes and was doing everything by, I don't know, sense of *smell* or something. I might as well admit it: I was just totally out of control. It didn't matter how many times I made the ship flip upside down, scoot sideways, or even blast backward at full speed. I was going to figure this thing out!

"More grull!" I shouted again and again.

The ship rocked. It lurched. It weaved and banked and did loop-the-loops. It spun from top to bottom. It spun from side to side. It spun from back to front and front to back and back to back and . . . *man*, did it ever spin.

But . . .

    . . . after a while . . .

        . . . it started to fly straight.

And somehow I actually began to get a feel for what worked and what didn't. It had nothing to do with thinking. It was like my hands were figuring out where to go on their own and my job was just to stay out of their way. My left hand pulled a knob: the engine boomed. My right hand hammered a button: the ship dipped and zoomed forward.

At one point I noticed Poog hovering just a few feet away from my right shoulder. He was smiling. I could see myself reflected in his big glassy eyes. I was smiling too.

The stars whizzed by.

The engine roared.

Now Streed's ship was in my sight. He was no more than a hundred yards ahead of us. My hands flew all over the dashboard: every lever I pulled brought us closer to Streed.

"More grull!" I cried.

Now we were just twenty yards behind him. Now fifteen. Now ten, now five.

I threw one last switch.

*GGGRRRREEEEAAAAAAARRR!*

Disaster! Our ship swerved to the left and was headed straight into Streed's exhaust fires. For a blinding second it looked as if we were going to plunge straight into his ship from behind. The windshield was a blaze of yellow-orange fire, the air rippling with heat.

I closed my eyes and gripped the dashboard with all my might, waiting for and dreading the impact of the crash. There was a horrific second of silence, then:

*FWUUUUUUUUM!*

Nothing but stars in front of us. Nothing but stars on both sides. Streed's ship was nowhere to be seen.

"Heavens, Akiko!" Mr. Beeba said, trotting up to the front of the ship, grull shovel in hand. "You . . ."

He paused and drew in his breath, the hint of a smile forming on his lips.

". . . you *bumped* him!"

"No way," I said.

"Oh yes."

"Really?"

"ABSOLUTELY," said Gax.

Yes.

*"Yes!"* I cried. "I bumped him, I *bumped* him!"

I wanted to jump up and dance, I was so happy. Mr. Beeba threw his arms around me and gave me a great big hug. Poog beamed and bobbed up and down.

Ozlips danced around and around and jumped into my lap. "Yish! Yish!" he said.

"Take *that*, Streed!" I shouted. "We're gonna win! We're gonna *win!*"

I was just about to ask Mr. Beeba to go wake Spuckler up and tell him the good news when Gax interrupted.

"MA'AM, I HATE TO THROW A DAMPER ON THE FESTIVITIES, BUT THE RACE IS NOT OVER YET. WE ARE NOW APPROACHING THE JAWS OF McVLUDDAPUCK."

# Chapter 16

**The Jaws of McVluddapuck.** I'd *completely* forgotten about them. There they were ahead in the distance: two enormous half-planets, each thousands of miles from top to bottom. Their outer surfaces were bright red, speckled with craters and vast deserts. The Jaws—the inner surfaces created when the planet split in half—were perfectly flat, smoothed by a million years of pounding into each other.

*throom*

*THROOM*

*THROOM*

The sound of the slamming Jaws thundered through the walls of our ship. It was the noise you'd hear if two mountains leaped into the air and rammed into each other.

For a moment I was frozen at the wheel, hypnotized by the two halves joining, separating, joining, once every seven seconds or so, just like Mr. Beeba had said. He was right. There was something elegant about it, something really beautiful.

*THROOM*

   *THROOM*

      *THROOM*

But if we were going to fly through the Jaws of McVluddapuck, one thing was sure: We'd need speed, and a *lot* of it.

"Sorry, Ozlips." I picked him up off my lap and dropped him to the floor. He whined a bit as he scampered away.

"Empty the grull bin, Mr. Beeba!" I shouted. "Throw it all into the furnace!"

"But—" said Mr. Beeba.

"We need *all* of it," I said.

"BUT—" said Gax.

*"All of it!"*

I turned my head to make sure Mr. Beeba was following orders. Sure enough, he was feverishly shoveling in the very last of the grull, causing white-hot towers of flame to burst from the furnace with every load. The engine roared as it received this final boost of energy, and the ship began to rattle and shake and hurl itself forward through the stars even faster than before.

*THROOM*

*THROOM*

*THROOOOM!*

I gazed through the windshield at the massive red sphere before us, splitting in half and slamming together again and again and again. Before long my entire field of vision was filled with the surface of the planet and the terrifyingly narrow gap that kept appearing and disappearing, appearing and disappearing.

*THROOOOOOOM!*

I had to get the timing right.

If we flew into the Jaws even a split second too late, we'd never make it through to the other side before it closed again. My hands were frozen on the acceleration levers. What to do? I knew we'd have to fly into the gap at top speed, but entering at precisely the right moment was crucial. Should we be going faster? Slower?

The gap opened.

We were still many miles away; even at its widest the gap looked incredibly narrow. It was going to be like driving a truck into an alley at a hundred miles an hour.

*THROOOOOOOOOOOM!*

The Jaws slammed closed again.

Our ship kept barreling in, closer, closer . . .

"YOUR TIMING IS OFF, MA'AM," said Gax, a staticky quiver in his voice. "WE'RE GOING TO HIT IT WHILE IT'S STILL CLOSED."

"Tell me what to do, Gax!" I shouted. *"Faster? Slower?"*

He didn't answer right away. His mechanical brain must have been doing cartwheels trying to come up with an accurate calculation.

The Jaws opened again. We were much closer now, and for a few seconds I could see clear through to the stars on the other side.

Light reflected off the massive interior walls before vanishing as the gap closed once again.

*THROOOOOOOOOOOM!*

"FASTER," said Gax.

"NO, SLOWER!" he said a second later.

"NO, WAIT, *FASTER!*"

*"Which is it?"* I screamed.

There was a high-pitched gurgle in my left ear.

"Poog says slower!" said Mr. Beeba.

I wiped the sweat from my eyes as the Jaws of McVluddapuck opened one more time. This was it. After they slammed shut, we needed to be right there when they opened again, ready to enter the gap the moment it reappeared.

I threw both of my hands around a lever in the middle of the dashboard—a braking mechanism—and pulled down with all my might. The ship screeched and howled.

*THROOOOOOOOOOOOOOOOOOOOOM!*

The gap was gone.

We were only seconds away from the surface, still careening toward a pathway that no longer existed. I pulled the lever as hard as I could, trying desperately to slow down. It was no use. *Boach's Bullet* was hurtling forward under its own momentum.

*GREEEEEEEEEEEEEEEE!*

The windshield was a sea of red, the surface of the planet now visible in terrifying stone-and-pebble detail. I braced myself for the impact. The crash was coming, it was all over. . . .

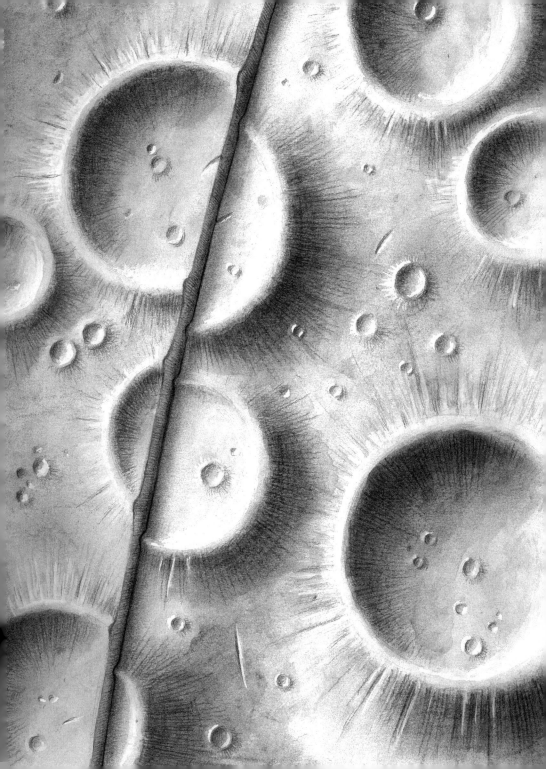

# Chapter 17

**FOOOOOOOOOSSSSHHHH**

We were inside the Jaws of McVluddapuck. The gap had reopened at the last possible moment and our ship was flying almost noiselessly through the increasingly wide passageway.

*FOOOOOOOOOOOOOOSSSSHHHH*

The shadowy red walls dissolved into a blur as we zoomed closer and closer to the stars on the other side. Everything seemed to be happening in slow motion. I knew we had only 7.3 seconds before the Jaws would close again. How many seconds had already passed? Two? Three?

"FOUR SECONDS," said Gax, as if reading my mind.

"The walls are closing in again!" I heard Mr. Beeba say. "We're not going to make it!"

*FOOOOOOOOOOOOOOSSSSHHHH*

I pulled the accelerator levers with all the strength I had inside me. The engines roared, incinerating the very last of the grull, and the ship rocketed forward at a truly terrifying speed. But the starry sliver of space ahead still seemed impossibly far away.

"FIVE SECONDS," said Gax.

By now I could practically feel the interior walls of McVluddapuck closing in around us. It looked like the wings of the ship had no more than a couple of yards of open space on either side. I had this terribly clear picture in my head of *Boach's Bullet* getting caught in the Jaws—how it would look from somewhere up above, sparks flaring as the red walls clamped onto the wings and ground the ship to a halt before crushing it like a tin can in a trash compactor.

"Sideways!" Mr. Beeba howled. "You've got to turn the ship sideways! It's the only way we'll make it through!"

I yanked knobs, pulled levers, hammered one button after another, but none of them did anything at all.

*FOOOOOOOOOOOOOOSSSSHHHH*

"SIX SECONDS," said Gax.

*TRIT-TRIT-TRIT-TRIT-TRIT-TRIT*

One of the ship's wings was skidding along the surface of the wall. Sparks were flying across the windshield like a yellow-orange snowstorm.

*"Siiidewaaaays!"* Mr. Beeba shrieked.

The ever-narrowing sliver of stars on the other side of McVluddapuck was at least a mile away. The ship's right-hand wing was being shaved down to a stub. Worst of all, we were now beginning to lose speed.

We'd never make it like this.

Giving up hope, I let go of the controls altogether, threw my hands over my eyes, and slammed my forehead down on the dashboard.

*FOOOOOOOOOOOOOOOOOOOOOO—*

Huh? We were still moving.

I raised my head and peered through my fingers.

The sparks were gone.

The ship had flipped sideways! I must have hit the right button with my forehead!

Faster, faster, faster . . .

"7.2 SECONDS," said Gax.

*—OOOOOSSSSSSSSSSHHHHHHHHHHHH!*

We shot out into the stars, the Jaws of McVluddapuck closing behind with a deafening clap of thunder.

*THRRROOOOOOOOOOOOOMMMMM*

127

Oh man. I wish you could have seen it: the hugging and dancing and hollering and just sheer joy that broke out on that ship. It had nothing to do with winning the race and everything to do with simply being alive!

I ran over to check on Spuckler and found to my delight that he'd been awake—groggy, but awake—through the whole thing.

He propped himself up on his elbows and asked me to kneel down beside him.

I did.

"That was darn good flyin', 'Kiko," he whispered. "*Darn* good."

"Thanks, Spuckler." I felt like I was about to cry. Was that a tear on Spuckler's cheek? No way!

"Now get back to the controls," he said, rubbing one eye. "We ain't crossed the finish line yet."

He was right, of course. But it wouldn't be long now. The Alpha Centauri Stadium was already coming into view. I jumped back to the driver's seat and reduced our speed, trying to conserve what little power we had left.

"Poog," I asked, "do you see Bluggamin Streed out there anywhere?"

Poog gurgled something in reply, which Mr. Beeba translated as "He's miles behind us. He mistimed the Jaws and had to circle back to have another go at it."

"I can't believe it," I said. "We're really going to win this thing! Gax, how's the Twerbo-Fladiator?"

"JUST FINE, MA'AM," he answered. "THE NEEDLE HASN'T BUDGED IN MORE THAN HALF AN HOUR."

"Really?" I said. "That's funny, it was overheating like *crazy* before."

The stadium was now only ten or twenty miles away. At our current pace we'd cross the finish line in just a couple of minutes. I checked my watch: 5 P.M. Perfect. I'd still have just enough time to get back for dinner at six. Heck, I could even push it until six-thirty if I really—

*FLAAM!*

*FLA-FLAAAAAAAAAM!*

Two loud noises—like explosions, almost—shook the ship from front to back. We continued moving forward and everything seemed to be okay. But a little red bulb on the dashboard started flashing and buzzing loudly.

"Heavens!" gasped Mr. Beeba. "The escape pod!"

"Escape pod?" I asked.

"All ships come equipped with escape pods, Akiko," he explained, pointing to a small round hatch on one wall surrounded by black and yellow stripes. "Well, except for *this* one, as of a few seconds ago."

"What, it just . . . shot out of the ship all by itself?"

"I'm afraid not, Akiko," said Mr. Beeba. "I'll lay odds a certain little friend of ours was on board."

I turned and looked around. Poog. Spuckler. Gax. Mr. Beeba. Everyone but . . .

*Ozlips.*

In all the excitement, I'd totally forgotten all about him. Sure enough, he was nowhere to be seen. But why would he leave us now, right when we were about to—

Whatever. It would have to wait. We were already zooming into Alpha Centauri Stadium, coasting on our last vapors of grull. I cut back on the accelerator and decided to take things slowly. This was a moment to savor!

The stadium was wide and round, a huge white space station lit by gigantic lamps hovering above it. The stands were filled with cheering crowds. A strange alien fanfare blared from speakers on all sides. Carved into the middle of the stadium was a long gray path like an airport runway. There at the far end was a shimmering golden ribbon: the finish line!

"Spuckler!" I cried. "Are you still awake?"

"I'm watchin', 'Kiko, I'm watchin'!"

We floated down to the foot of the runway and began our slow flight to victory.

*FFFFFSSSSSSSSSSSHHHHHHHHH*

A loud hissing filled the ship.

"MALFUNCTION!" said Gax. "THE . . . THE TWERBO-FLADIATOR IS OVERHEATING!"

I shot a glance over my shoulder. Thick black smoke was pouring out of the thing. The Lava lamp part looked like it was actually on fire.

I got an awful, queasy feeling in my stomach as I remembered the tiny crack I'd made when I dropped it.

"Dagnabbit, Gax," Spuckler cried, "I thought you was keepin' an eye on that gauge!"

"I WAS, SIR!" Gax protested. "I . . . I . . ."

It was the first time I'd heard Gax at a loss for words.

I turned back to face the finish line, now just fifty feet away. We were still moving forward. At a snail's pace. But *still moving.*

Spuckler rose to his feet. "We're losin' altitude. Better put down the landin' gear, 'Kiko. That black knob there on the right."

I yanked it hard. The ship shook a bit as the wheels descended from their compartments beneath us. Were we really going to have to *roll* to the finish line like some old jalopy? Come on!

"Don't worry, everybody," I said. "We're almost there. We're still going to win."

*PLAM! PLAM! PLA-PLAAM!*

The Twerbo-Fladiator exploded, sending shards of metal and glass ricocheting all around us. Our ship dropped to the runway with a sickening crash. The finish line was only twenty feet ahead of us. If we could just keep moving . . .

*FLOOOOOOOOOOOOOOOOOOOOOOM!*

The engine gave out a terrific boom and then fell utterly silent. All the lights on the dashboard went out, and even the ceiling lights dimmed to a yellowish flicker. It felt like we were trapped inside a dying animal.

The wheels carried us forward a few more feet . . .

. . . a few more inches . . .

. . . then squealed to a halt.

The finish line was ten feet away.

"No!" I cried. "This can't be happening!"

The ship was filled with the roar of the crowd outside. What were they *cheering* about? Were they crazy?

Then we heard it. A high-pitched engine roar in the distance behind our ship.

"Dag . . . ," Spuckler cried, ". . . *nabbit!*"

The crowd went wild as Streed's ship shot by—bumping us one last time—and zoomed across the finish line.

The Alpha Centauri 5000 was over.

Streed had won.

# Chapter 18

**It was like a bad dream.** How could we have come so close and then lost?

Music blared. People cheered. Through the windshield I could see Streed climb out of his ship and into a swarm of alien news reporters. A second ship shot by. Then a third and a fourth. And there we were, still ten feet away from the finish line.

I felt like crying. I also felt like kicking something.

"It's not fair!" I slammed my fists down on the dashboard over and over. "It's just not fair!"

"Take it easy, now, 'Kiko," I heard Spuckler say. "Ya did yer best. It ain't your fault."

"It *is* my fault! I dropped the Twerbo-Fladiator and broke it! I know I should have told you all, but—"

"Hang on a second, 'Kiko," Spuckler said. "I've dropped that thing dozensa times. You couldn'ta broke it all by yourself. It ain't as fragile as that."

"I did, though! I did!" Now I really *was* crying. "I dropped it and the glass cracked and now we've lost the race! It *is* my fault. It *is*. . . ."

Mr. Beeba stepped forward and cleared his throat. "Oh, but it's not as simple as that, my dear girl." He was holding what remained of the Twerbo-Fladiator. "It was not a matter of a crack in the glass. It was a matter of this."

He reached underneath and pulled out a small black box. It looked like it had been attached with some sort of putty.

"Sabotage!"

Spuckler squinted. Gax rattled. Poog looked sad, but not at all surprised.

"I knew it. I *knew* it," said Spuckler. "That little varmint!"

"Ozlips," said Mr. Beeba.

"*Ozlips?*" I said. "You mean—"

"It all seems so clear now. He came aboard this ship for one reason and one reason only: to prevent us from winning."

"But—"

"Disabling the Twerbo-Fladiator must have been plan B." Mr. Beeba stepped over to Spuckler's side. "Show us the back of your neck, Spuckler."

Spuckler turned and pulled his straggly blue hair up against the back of his head. There, in the exact center of his neck, was a reddish circular mark with a bright red dot in the middle.

"Plan A," said Mr. Beeba. "Knock Spuckler out so that he can no longer fly the ship properly. The little chap must have injected you with a tiny dose of Somnus-Ether when he was cleaning off the black-hole mucus. Just enough to knock you out until the end of the race."

It couldn't have happened that way. It just didn't seem possible.

"But why?" I asked. "Why would he *do* this to us? He should be grateful. We . . . we helped him escape from his master!"

"Ya wanna see that critter's master?" said Spuckler, pointing a finger toward the windshield. "He's standin' right over there."

I whirled around and stared through the glass, fully expecting to see some big mean ogre of a man with a whip. Instead, my eyes fell on Bluggamin Streed. He was standing on the winner's platform, the Centauri Cup in one arm, posing for photo after photo. And there, perched on his shoulder, was Ozlips: smiling and laughing, clearly enjoying all the attention.

"They tricked us," Spuckler said. "Tricked us fair and square."

"Fair?" I said. "Are you nuts? Sabotage isn't fair!"

"Everything's fair in the Alpha Centauri 5000, 'Kiko." Spuckler sat down and grinned. "Even cheatin'. Some people do it. Some people don't."

Unbelievable.

"Me, I don't go for cheatin'. It just don't *feel* right to me. Plus I ain't got the smarts to pull it off."

Mr. Beeba nodded his agreement. Gax and Poog nodded right along with him.

I was stunned. How could they be so calm about losing? The least they could do was be as angry as me.

"You . . . you guys don't even *care*, do you?"

"I care. I care plenty." Spuckler took my hand in his. "What I care about is how well we ran that race, 'Kiko. And we ran it better than all the rest of those lunkheads put together. Lots better."

"Let me get this straight. You're saying . . . basically . . . that it's not whether you win or lose, it's how you play the game."

Mr. Beeba beamed.

"That's a *splendid* way of putting it, Akiko. Is that one of your own?"

"It's how ya play the game," repeated Spuckler. "That's right, you got the gist of it there, 'Kiko. So we never made it 'cross the finish line. We gave it our best shot, an' we had a darned good time. What's the big deal?"

I was speechless. Well, for a few seconds, anyway.

"You want to know what the big deal is? This is the big deal: I just went through the most terrifying Saturday in *history*."

I was shaking with anger. I started pacing back and forth, chopping at the air as I tried to get the words out. "Trans-Moovulators! Asteroids! Black holes! The, the, the—"

"JAWS OF McVLUDDAPUCK?" Gax offered.

"McVluddapuck? Try Mc-*DEATH*-apuck! I nearly got killed about *seventeen times* today, and, and, and, and I'm not going to let some cheater go home with *my* trophy!"

"But 'Kiko—"

"Don't try to calm me down!" I was stomping back and forth, throwing my arms all over the place. "Cheating's okay? What are you going to tell me next? Losing is cool? Losing is fun?"

Mr. Beeba coughed. "Well, it *does* have a certain noble quality to it, Akiko, you have to admit."

"I don't have to admit anything!" I pointed a finger at Mr. Beeba that nearly touched his nose. "Losing is *not* cool! Or fun! Or noble! Losing stinks! Losing is . . . for losers!"

Everyone stared at me. They looked frightened.

There was a noise.

Outside.

Coming from the stands.

It sounded like a small group of spectators were shouting something in unison, some sort of cheer. More and more joined in each time they repeated the phrase. It grew louder and louder, clearer and clearer.

"The Rusty Sprocket," said Mr. Beeba. "I'd almost forgotten."

"That's right!" Spuckler snapped his fingers. "We still got a chance at it!"

"The rusty *what?*"

"It's an award they give out," Mr. Beeba explained, "to the last person to cross the finish line. A sort of consolation prize."

The cheering outside was getting even louder, almost frantic.

"C'mon, everybody!" Spuckler hollered as he threw open the door. "We gotta push this sucker 'cross the finish line!"

Spuckler leaped out of the ship, followed by Gax, Poog, and Mr. Beeba.

I was still pretty angry. *Very* angry, actually. But I couldn't just stand there alone while everyone else left the ship. So I got out.

And we all started pushing.

# Chapter 19

**All three tires** were completely flat. But with everyone pushing—and I mean everyone, even Poog—the ship began to roll forward, one squeaky inch at a time.

The crowd was going wild. They actually seemed more excited about us winning the Rusty Sprocket than about Streed winning the Centauri Cup.

*"Dzu! Dzu! Dzu! Dzu! Dzu!"*

They shouted just one word over and over again. I figure it meant *go* or *fight* or something like that. Whatever it meant, it did the job: My arms and legs were charged up with so much energy, it felt like electricity flowing through me. I heaved myself up against the back of the ship and pushed with every last bit of strength I had left. The wheels screeched. The crowds

roared. Sweat covered everything: my face, my back, my belly. The cheers were deafening. I gritted my teeth and pushed even harder.

Finally the crowd exploded in celebration: Our ship's nose had inched across the finish line. The Rusty Sprocket was ours.

Alien spectators leaped out of the stands and flooded around us. They took photos. They asked for autographs. They offered handshakes—or tentacle-shakes, in some cases—and thumped us hard on our backs.

Okay, so we came in last. It sure *felt* like we won.

Everything that happened after that is a bit of a blur. A really *nice* blur. There was punch to drink and tables piled high with food (no horb-noks, thank goodness) and nice soft chairs to lean back in. People and aliens and all sorts of creatures in between kept coming up to congratulate us and view the Rusty Sprocket trophy, which was actually pretty cool: a wide black base with two rust-colored cogs hovering above it with their teeth interlocked, spinning slowly in midair.

The low point for me was when Bluggamin Streed, Ozlips still on his shoulder, came over to congratulate

us. I wanted to punch both of them right in the nose. But Spuckler was chatting almost like they were old friends.

"Ya got me there, Bluggy," he said. "I shoulda known you'd try'n' pull somethin' like that."

Ozlips gave me a wink. I turned away.

Streed placed the Centauri Cup on a table and used it as a prop for his elbow. The big golden trophy was shaped like a rocket ship and sparkled like nothing I'd ever seen.

"I keep telling you, Boach. You'll never win a race until you get rid of two things: your stinky old grull, and your outdated 'no cheating' code of ethics."

"Cheatin's for sissies, Bluggy," Spuckler said. "And winnin' ain't everything."

"It's the *only* thing," said Streed.

"'Kiko here's got a better one: It ain't whether you win or lose . . ." He paused and turned to me. "How's the rest of that go?"

146

"Forget it, Spuckler," I said, still facing away from all three of them. "They wouldn't understand."

"Yeah, I reckon you're right about that, 'Kiko."

"So long, Spuck," said Streed as he and Ozlips disappeared into the crowds. "See you at the next one."

"Sassy little punk," said Spuckler. He swigged down the last of a cup of punch. "Kinda like *me*, come to think of it."

Now it was time for repairs. Spuckler went off and came back with a brand-new Twerbo-Fladiator and a fresh supply of coolant to go with it. He sang one last song as he and Gax set to work. This one had the exact same melody as the other two but was somehow even more irritating. It was all about something called grixel oil.

*"Oh, grixel oil, grixel oil,*
*It saves ya time and it saves ya toil,*
*I loves it more than I loves my goyyyyyyyyyyyl . . ."*
You get the idea.

By the time he was finished, I was beginning to worry about how long I'd been away from Earth. It was already quarter after six: I was now officially late for dinner.

# Chapter 20

**It took us about an hour** to get back to Earth. Spuckler offered to take the controls, but I told him to sit down. I wasn't going to pass up my last chance to fly *Boach's Bullet*. I'd kind of grown attached to the old thing.

I steered us past galaxy after galaxy, under large spinning planets and over oceans of asteroids, until finally we arrived in the Milky Way, hung a left at Jupiter, and zoomed straight over to the third planet from the sun.

I pulled *Boach's Bullet* up to a spot near the moon, unbuckled my safety belts, and stepped over to the Trans-Moovulator. Mr. Beeba helped me put my coat back on.

"I thought you didn't *like* being Trans-Moovulated, Akiko," he said.

"I don't," I said. "But I can't have anyone see me stepping out of this spaceship in the middle of Middleton Park. I've got enough problems at school without kids thinking I've been abducted by aliens."

"But you *have* been abducted by aliens."

I grinned. "Really goofy ones too."

Spuckler shook my hand. *"Boach's Bullet* ain't never had a better pilot than you, 'Kiko. The Jaws of McVluddapuck in 7.2 seconds? Even *I'm* not crazy enough to try that."

"WHAT WILL YOU TELL YOUR PARENTS, MA'AM,"

asked Gax, "WHEN THEY ASK WHY YOU WERE LATE FOR DINNER?"

"I'll just say I accidentally locked myself in the girls' bathroom at the library," I said. "I did that once before. They might buy it."

Poog floated forward and smiled. I gave him a big hug.

"Thanks for getting us through the Labyrinth of Lulla-ma-Waygo, Poog," I said. "If only you had arms and legs, I'll bet you'd be able to fly this ship better than anybody." I paused and added: "Forget I said that. You'd look really *weird* with arms and legs."

I zipped up my coat, stepped onto the scuff-marked gray square, and turned to Mr. Beeba.

"If you push the wrong button and beam me to Neptune I'm going to kill you."

"*Trans-Moovulate*, Akiko. Trans-Moovulate."

I smiled.

"Don't mind if I do."


"Guess where I went yesterday."

It was Sunday afternoon. Melissa and I were hanging around in my bedroom, looking at magazines.

"I don't know," I said. "Where?"

"The new mall in Fowlerville." The way Melissa said it, you'd think she'd spent the day in heaven. "You have *got* to get your parents to take you there, Akiko. It's the best. There's every kind of store you can imagine, and there's this play area with, like, a mini–roller coaster. Right there in the mall. And the food court . . ."

She went on like that for probably twenty minutes. I tried to look interested, I really did. But I was remembering my own adventure from the day before. I was lucky. I'd forgotten that my parents had had this thing to go to on Saturday afternoon. A string quartet in Leamington, followed by a buffet dinner or something. They got home about eight o'clock. Ten minutes after I'd dashed back to the apartment, let myself in, and scarfed down the lasagna—cold—that my mom had left for me in the refrigerator.

"So what did you do yesterday?"

Melissa was staring at me. I'd almost missed the question.

"Me?"

"Yes, you." She rolled her eyes. "Yesterday, after I left you in the park. What did you do?"

Oh, not much. Just got Trans-Moovulated, that's all.
"Built a snowman," I said.

My mind kept drifting back to the Alpha Centauri 5000 and everything that came with it: the horrible smell of grull, the tooth-rattling rumble of the engine, Spuckler's awful songs. The funny thing was, I knew I would miss it all someday. Heck, I was starting to miss it already.

Melissa tossed her magazine aside and grabbed another. "You spent the whole afternoon building a snowman."

"Sure."

"One snowman?"

"Uh-huh."

Clouds moved out of the sun's way and the whole room lit up. I rolled over onto my stomach so my back could get warm.

Melissa shook her head.

"Akiko," she said.

"What?"

"You have *got* to get out of Middleton."

**Mark Crilley** was raised in Detroit, where he never had the opportunity to get behind the controls of a spaceship (but once popped a wheelie on his bicycle for nearly 7.2 seconds). After graduating from Kalamazoo College in 1988, he traveled to Taiwan and Japan, where he taught English to students of all ages for nearly five years. It was during his stay in Japan in 1992 that he created the story of Akiko and her journey to the planet Smoo. First published as a comic book in 1995, the bimonthly Akiko series has since earned Crilley numerous award nominations, as well as a spot on *Entertainment Weekly*'s "It List" in 1998. Crilley lives with his wife, Miki, and son, Matthew, just a few miles from the streets where he was raised.